FANNY HILL

Unknown: Madame Modeste

FANNY HILL

Memoirs of a Woman of Pleasure

John Cleland

Introduction by Neil Philip

PARRAGON

This abridged but unexpurgated edition first published
in Great Britain in 1989 by
Sidgwick & Jackson Limited

This edition produced by Carlton Books for Parragon Book Service

An Albion Book

ISBN 1 85813 199 5

Printed by Toppan

Introduction

Fanny Hill is a clandestine classic. For years much sought after for its reputation as, in James Boswell's words, a 'most licentious and inflaming book', it is now recognized as a vigorous comic novel in the tradition of Defoe, Richardson, Fielding and Smollett. Its great achievement is its robust and good-humoured heroine, who turns every adversity to her advantage in her rise through harlotry to riches and respectability. Fanny, it has been said, is 'halfway between Moll Flanders and Molly Bloom'; her easy virtue is a deliberate mockery of the *vartue* of Richardson's Pamela.

The book was first published, under its official title *Memoirs of a Woman of Pleasure*, in 1748-9, and quickly suppressed, only to reappear in edition after edition, and language after language, from then to the present day. Its author, John Cleland, wrote or rewrote it while imprisoned for debt. He later disowned it as 'a Book I disdain to defend, and wish, from my Soul, buried and forgot', but for good or ill it is the work on which his reputation rests.

Cleland was born in 1710, the first son of a Scots army officer of comfortable means. For some reason, he did not pursue the expected course for a young man of his class, but left school at the age of twelve, and five years later departed for India as a private soldier. In India he had a successful career as an employee of the East India Company, returning to England on his father's death in 1741. From then on, he scraped a living as a Grub Street hack, reduced more than once, as in 1748, to debtors' prison. After *Fanny Hill* he published novels, dramas, poems, linguistic studies, political journalism, with the measure of success suggested by Boswell's description of his room in old age, 'filled with books in confusion and dust'. He died in 1789.

While *Fanny Hill* is deliberately in the tradition of the French erotic novels which were widely read in eighteenth-century England, it has many original features, most notably the rococo extravagance of its prose, with its marvellous array of apt metaphor and simile. Another point which must strike every reader is the realism of its incidental detail. The obvious comparison is to the contemporary engravings of William Hogarth: many writers have noted that an apt title for Cleland's novel would be that used by

Hogarth for a series of engravings in 1732, 'The Harlot's Progress'. But there is a key difference. While Hogarth's Moll Hackabout sinks into misery, disease and degradation, Cleland's Fanny ends up happy and prosperous.

Both Hogarth and Cleland's plot-lines could be paralleled in the London of their day. Prostitution was rife in eighteenth-century London. As one ballad of 1744 puts it:

> Honest Women there is few, Jilts there is many.
> At every corner of the street there's Whores eight o'Penny.

Rakes could even buy a guide to the whores of Covent Garden. Some of these women found fame and fortune, such as the courtesan Kitty Fisher, who was painted by Reynolds and became the mistress of the Duke of York. But for every Kitty Fisher there must have been many abused unhappy girls whose squalid lives can be glimpsed in a ballad such as 'The Poor Whores Complaint':

> Come listen a while and you shall hear,
> How the poor Whores fares in the winter
> They've hardly got any rags to hide their ware
> Indeed tis a despret thing, Sir.
> With their draggel tales thats nine inches deep,
> And hardly a shoe or a stocking,
> Yet if a Cull they by chance should meet,
> At him they will be bobing.

A customer's eye view of London's prostitutes later in the century is provided by James Boswell, who is also one of the most interesting witnesses to Cleland's old age. A typical passage of Boswell's *London Journal* tells us:

> 25 March 1763 – As I was coming home this night, I felt carnal inclinations raging through my frame. I determined to gratify them. I went to St James Park and picked up a whore. For the first time did I engage in armour (i.e. a sheath) which I found but dull satisfaction. She who submitted to my lusty embraces was a young Shropshire girl, only 17, very well-looked, her name Elizabeth Parker. Poor being, she has a sad time of it!

Beside the streets and public parks, there were bagnios and fashionable brothels to cater for all tastes and pockets.

John Cleland's own sexual tastes are a mystery. He never married, and it was rumoured, perhaps maliciously, that he was homosexual. But he was clearly familiar with London's sexual underworld, and was writing for an audience which itself patronised and sustained the endless round of sexual commerce. *Fanny Hill*, while perhaps not, as Fanny claims, 'Truth! stark naked truth', depicts a world which really existed.

But enough: let Fanny tell her own story.

Neil Philip

Thomas Rowlandson: Peg Woffinton

Part One

Madam,

I sit down to give you an undeniable proof of my considering your desires as indispensible orders: ungracious then as the task may be, I shall recall to view those scandalous stages of my life, out of which I emerged at length, to the enjoyment of every blessing in the power of love, health, and fortune to bestow, whilst yet in the flower of youth, and not too late to employ the leisure afforded me by great ease and affluence, to cultivate an understanding naturally not a despicable one, and which had, even amidst the whirl of loose pleasures I had been tossed in, exerted more observation on the characters and manners of the world than what is common to those of my unhappy profession, who, looking on all thought or reflection as their capital enemy, keep it at as great a distance as they can, or destroy it without mercy.

Hating, as I mortally do, all long unnecessary prefaces, I shall give you good quarter in this, and use no farther apology than to prepare you for seeing the loose part of my life, wrote with the same liberty that I led it.

Truth! stark naked truth, is the word, and I will not so much as take the pains to bestow the strip of a gauze-wrapper on it, but paint situations such as they actually rose to me in nature, careless of violating those laws of decency, that were never made for such unreserved intimacies as ours: and you have too much sense, too much knowledge of the *originals* themselves, to snuff prudishly and out of character at the *pictures* of them. The greatest men, those of the first and most leading taste, will not scruple adorning their private closets with nudities, though, in compliance with vulgar prejudices they may not think them decent decorations of the staircase or saloon.

This and enough premised, I go souse into my personal history. My maiden name was Frances Hill. I was born at a small village near Liverpool in Lancashire, of parents extremely poor, and, I piously believe, extremely honest.

My father, who had received a maim on his limbs that disabled him from following the more laborious branches of country-drudgery, got, by making of nets, a scanty subsistance, which was not much enlarged by my mother's keeping a little day-school for the girls in her neighbourhood. They had had several children, but none lived to any age, except myself, who had received from nature a constitution perfectly healthy.

Rowlandson: The Ogler

My education, till past fourteen, was no better than very vulgar; reading, or rather spelling, an illegible scrawl, and a little ordinary plainwork, composed the whole system of it: and then all my foundation in virtue was no other than a total ignorance of vice, and the shy timidity general to our sex, in the tender stage of life when objects alarm or frighten more by their novelty than any thing else: but then this is a fear too often cured at the expense of innocence, when Miss, by degrees, begins no longer to look on man as a creature of prey that will eat her.

My poor mother had divided her time so entirely between her scholars and her little domestic cares that she had spared very little of it to my instruction, having, from her own innocence from all ill, no hint or thought of guarding me against any.

I was now entering on my fifteenth year, when the worst of ills befell me in the loss of my tender fond parents, who were both carried off by the smallpox, within a few days of each other; my father dying first, and thereby hastening the death of my mother, so that I was now left an unhappy friendless Orphan: (for my father's coming to settle there was accidental, he being originally a Kentish-man). That cruel distemper which had proved so fatal to them had indeed seized me, but with such mild and favourable symptoms that I was presently out of danger, and, what I then did not know the value of, was entirely unmarked. I skip over here an account of the natural grief and affliction which I felt on this melancholy occasion. A little time, and the giddiness of that age, dissipated too soon my reflections on that irreparable loss; but nothing contributed more to reconcile me to it than the notions that were immediately put into my head of going to London and looking out for a service, in which I was promised all assistance and advice, from one Esther Davis, a young woman that had been down to see her friends and who, after the stay of a few days, was to return to her place.

As I had now nobody left alive in the village who had concern enough about what should become of me to start any objections to this scheme, and the woman who took care of me after my parents' death rather encouraged me to pursue it, I soon came to a resolution of making this launch into the wide world by repairing to London in order to seek my fortune, a phrase which, by the bye, has ruined more adventurers of both sexes, from the country, than ever it made or advanced.

Nor did Esther Davis a little comfort and inspirit me to venture with her by piquing my childish curiosity with the fine sights that were to be seen in London: the tombs, the lions, the king, the royal family, the fine plays and operas, and, in short, all the diversions which fell within her sphere of life to come at, the detail of all which perfectly turned the little head of me.

Nor can I remember, without laughing, the innocent admiration, not without a spice of envy, with which we poor girls, whose church-going clothes did not rise above dowlass shifts and stuff gowns, beheld Esther's scowered satin-gown, caps bordered with an inch of lace, tawdry ribbons, and shoes belaced with silver! All which we imagined grew in London and entered for a great deal into my determination of trying to come in for my share of them.

The idea, however, of having the company of a townswoman with her was the trivial and all the motive that engaged Esther to take charge of me during my journey to town, where she told me, after her manner and style as how several maids out of the country had made themselves and all their kin forever, that by preserving their *Vartue*, some had taken so with their masters that they had married them, and kept them coaches and lived vastly grand and happy and some, mayhap, came to be duchesses. Luck was all and why not I as well as another, with other almanacs to this purpose which set me a tiptoe to begin this promising journey, and to leave a place which, though my native one, contained no relations that I had reason to regret and was grown insupportable to me from the change of the tenderest usage into a cold air of charity with which I was entertained even at the only friend's house that I had the least expectations of care and protection from. She was, however, so just to me as to manage the turning into money the little matters that remained to me after the debts and burial-charges were accounted for and at my departure put my whole fortune into my hands, which consisted of a very slender wardrobe packed up in a very portable box and eight guineas with seventeen shillings in silver, stowed in a spring pouch which was a greater treasure than ever I had yet seen together and which I could not conceive there was a possibility of running out and indeed I was so entirely taken up with the joy of seeing myself mistress of such an immense sum that I gave very little attention to a world of good advice which was given me with it.

Places then being taken for Esther and me in the Chester-Waggon, I pass over a very immaterial scene of leave taking at which I dropt a few tears betwixt grief and joy; and, for the same reasons of insignificance, skip over all that happened to me on the road, such as the Waggoner's looking liquorish on me, the schemes laid for me by some of the passengers, which were defeated by the vigilance of my guardian Esther who, to do her justice, took a motherly care of me, at the same time that she taxed me for her protection by making me bear all travelling charges, which I defrayed with the utmost cheerfulness, and thought myself much obliged to her into the bargain. She took indeed great care that we were not over-rated or imposed on, as well as of managing as frugally as possible: expensiveness was not her vice.

It was pretty late in a summer evening when we reached the town, in our slow conveyance, though drawn by six at length. As we passed through the greatest streets that led to our inn, the noise of the coaches, the hurry, the crowds of foot passengers, in short, the new scenery of the shops and houses at once pleased and amazed me.

But guess at my mortification and surprise when we came to the inn, and our things were landed, and delivered to us, when my fellow traveller and

Thomas Rowlandson: Loading a Stage Coach (*detail*)

protectress, Esther Davis, who had used me with the utmost tenderness during the journey, and prepared me by no preceding signs for the stunning blow I was to receive, when, I say, my only dependance and friend, in this strange place, all of a sudden assumed a strange and cool air towards me, as if she dreaded my becoming a burden to her.

Instead then of proffering me the continuance of her assistance and good offices, which I relied upon and never more wanted, she thought herself, it seems, abundantly acquitted of her engagements to me by having brought me safe to my journey's end; and seeing nothing in her procedure towards me but what was natural and in order, began to embrace me by way of taking leave, whilst I was so confounded, so struck, that I had not spirit or sense enough so much as to mention my hopes or expectations from her experience and knowledge of the place she had brought me to.

Whilst I stood thus stupid and mute, which she doubtless attributed to nothing more than a concern at parting, this idea procured me perhaps a slight alleviation of it in the following harangue: that now we were got safe to London and that she was obliged to go to her place, she advised me by all means to get into one as soon as possible – that I need not fear getting one – there were more places than parish-churches – that she advised me to go to an intelligence office – that if she heard of anything stirring, she would find me out and let me know; that in the mean time I should take a private lodging and acquaint her where to send to me, that she wished me good luck and hoped I should always have the grace to keep myself honest and not bring a disgrace on my parentage. With this she took her leave of me and left me, as it were, on my own hands, full as lightly as I had been put into hers.

Left thus alone, absolutely destitute and friendless, I began then to feel most bitterly the severity of this separation, the scene of which had passed in a little room in the inn; and no sooner was her back turned, but the affliction I felt at my helpless strange circumstances burst out into a flood of tears, which infinitely relieved the oppression of my heart though I still remained stupified and most perfectly perplexed how to dispose of myself.

One of the drawers coming in added yet more to my uncertainty by asking me, in a short way, if I called for anything. To which I replied, innocently, 'no', but I wished him to tell me where I might get a lodging for that night. He said he would go and speak to his mistress, who accordingly came and told me drily, without entering in the least into the distress she saw me in, that I might have a bed for a shilling and that, as she supposed I had some friends in

Hogarth: The Harlot's Progress, plate 1

town (here I fetched a deep sigh in vain!) I might provide for myself in the morning.

It is incredible what trifling consolations the human mind will seize in its greatest afflictions. The assurance of nothing more than a bed to lie on that night calmed my agonies; and being ashamed to acquaint the mistress of the inn that I had no friends to apply to in town, I proposed to myself to proceed, the very next morning, to an intelligence office, to which I was furnished with written directions on the back of a ballad Esther had given me. There I counted on getting information of any place that such a country girl as I might be fit for, and where I could get into any sort of being before my little stock should be consumed. And as to a character, Esther had often repeated to me that I might depend on her managing me one; nor, however affected I was at her leaving me thus, did I entirely cease to rely on her, as I began to think good-naturedly that her procedure was all in course, and that it was only my ignorance of life that had made me take it in the light I at first did.

Accordingly, the next morning I dressed as clean and as neat as my rustic wardrobe would permit me; and having left my box, with special recommendation to the landlady, I ventured out by myself, and without any more difficulty than may be supposed of a young country girl, barely fifteen, and to whom every sign or shop was a gazing trap, I got to the wished-for intelligence office.

It was kept by an elderly woman who sat at the receipt of custom, with a book before her, in great form and order, and several scrolls, ready made out, of directions for places.

I made up then to this important personage, without lifting up my eyes or observing any of the people round me who were attending there on the same errand as myself, and dropping her curtsies nine deep, made just a shift to stammer out my business to her.

Madam having heard me out, with all the gravity and brow of a petty minister of state, and seeing, at one glance over my figure, what I was, made me no answer but to ask me the preliminary shilling, on receipt of which she told me places for women were exceeding scarce, especially as I seemed too slightly built for hard work but that she would look over her book and see what was to be done for me, desiring me to stay a little till she had dispatched some other customers.

On this, I drew back a little, most heartily mortified at a declaration which carried with it a killing uncertainty that my circumstances could not well endure.

Presently, assuming more courage and seeking some diversion from my uneasy thoughts, I ventured to lift up my head a little and sent my eyes on a course round the room where they met full tilt with those of a lady (for such my extreme innocence pronounced her) sitting in a corner of the room, dressed in a velvet manteel (*nota bene*, in the midst of summer) with her bonnet off; squob-fat, red-faced, and at least fifty.

She looked as if she would devour me with her eyes, staring at me from head to foot, without the least regard to the confusion and blushes her eyeing me so fixedly put me to and which were to her, no doubt, the strongest recommendation and marks of my being fit for her purpose. After a little time, in which my air, person, and whole figure had undergone her strict examination, which I had, on my part, tried to render favourable to me by primming, drawing up my neck, and setting my best looks, she advanced and spoke to me with the greatest demureness:

'Sweetheart, do you want a place?'

'Yes! and please you' (with a curtsy down to the ground).

Upon this she acquainted me that she was actually come to the office herself to look out for a servant, that she believed I might do, with a little of her instructions; that she could take my very looks for a sufficient character, that London was a very wicked, vile place, that she hoped I would be tractable and keep out of bad company. In short, she said all to me that an old experienced practitioner in town could think of and which was much more than was necessary to take in an artless inexperienced country maid, who was even afraid of becoming a wanderer about the streets and therefore gladly jumped at the first offer of a shelter, especially from so grave and matron-like a lady for such my flattering fancy assured me this now mistress of mine was: I being actually hired under the nose of the good woman that kept the office, whose shrewd smiles and shrugs I could not help observing, and innocently interpreted them as marks of her being pleased at my getting into place so soon: but, as I afterwards came to know, these beldams understood one another very well, and this was a market where Mrs Brown, my mistress, frequently attended on the watch for any fresh goods that might offer there, for the use of her customers and her own profit.

Madam was, however, so well pleased with her bargain, that fearing, I presume, lest better advice or some accident might occasion my slipping through her fingers, she would officiously take me in a coach to my inn where, calling herself for my box, it was, I being present, delivered without the least scruple or explanation as to where I was going.

This being over, she bid the coachman drive to a shop in St Paul's Churchyard, where she bought a pair of gloves, which she gave me and thence renewed her directions to the coachman to drive to her house in — street, who accordingly landed us at her door, after I had been cheered up and entertained by the way with the most plausible flams, without one syllable from which I could conclude anything but that I was by the greatest good luck fallen into the hands of the kindest mistress, not to say friend, that the varsal world could afford; and accordingly I entered her doors with most complete confidence and exultation, promising myself that, as soon as I should be a little settled, I would acquaint Esther Davis with my rare good fortune.

You may be sure the good opinion of my place was not lessened by the appearance of a very handsome back-parlour, into which I was led, and which seemed to me magnificently furnished, who had never seen better

Boitard: A Tailor's Shop (detail)

rooms than the ordinary ones in inns upon the road. There were two gilt pier-glasses, and a buffet in which a few pieces of plate, set out to the most show, dazzled and altogether persuaded me that I must be got into a very reputable family.

Here my mistress first began her part with telling me that I must have good spirits and learn to be free with her; that she had not taken me to be a common servant, to do domestic drudgery, but to be a kind of companion to her; and that, if I would be a good girl, she would do more than twenty mothers for me; to all which I answered only by the profoundest and the awkwardest curtsies and a few monosyllables, such as 'yes! no! to be sure'.

Presently my mistress touched the bell, and in came a strapping maid-servant who had let us in: 'Here, Martha,' said Mrs Brown, 'I have just hired this young woman to look after my linen, so step up and show her her chamber; and I charge you to use her with as much respect as you would myself, for I have taken a prodigious liking to her, and I do not know what I shall do for her.'

Martha, who was an arch jade, and being used to this decoy, had her cue perfect, made me a kind of half-curtsy and asked me to walk up with her and accordingly showed me a neat room, two pair of stairs backwards, in which there was a handsome bed where Martha told me I was to lie with a young gentlewoman, a cousin of my mistress's, who she was sure would be vastly good to me. Then she ran out into such affected encomiums on her good mistress! her sweet mistress! and how happy I was to light upon her, that I could not have bespoke a better, with other the like gross stuff, such as would itself have started suspicions in any but such an unpractised simpleton who was perfectly new to life and who took every word she said in the very sense she laid out for me to take it; but she readily saw what a penetration she had to deal with and measured me very rightly in her manner of whistling to me, so as to make me pleased with my cage and blind to its wires.

In the midst of these false explanations of the nature of my future service we were rung for down again, and I was reintroduced into the same parlour where there was a table laid with three covers; and my mistress had now got with her one of her favourite girls, a notable manager of her house, and whose business it was to prepare and break such young fillies as I was to the mounting block: and she was accordingly, in that view, allotted me for a bedfellow; and to give her the more authority, she had the title of cousin conferred on her by the venerable president of this college.

Here I underwent a second survey, which ended in the full approbation of Mrs Phoebe Ayres, the name of my tutoress elect, to whose care and instructions I was affectionately recommended.

Dinner was now set on the table, and in pursuance of treating me as a companion, Mrs Brown, with a tone to cut off all dispute, soon overruled all my most humble and confused protestations against sitting down with her Ladyship, which my very short breeding just suggested to me could not be right or in the order of things.

At table, the conversation was chiefly kept up by the two madams and carried on in double-meaning expressions, interrupted every now and then by kind assurances to me, all tending to confirm and fix my satisfaction with my present condition; augment it they could not, so very a novice was I then.

It was here agreed that I should keep myself up and out of sight for a few days, till such clothes could be procured for me as were fit for the character I was to appear in, of my mistress's companion, observing withall that on the first impressions of my figure much might depend; and, as they well judged, the prospect of exchanging my country clothes for the London finery made the clause of confinement digest perfectly well with me. But the truth was Mrs Brown did not care that I should be seen or talked to by any, either of her customers or her does, (as they called the girls provided for them) till she had secured a good market for my maidenhead, which I had at least all the appearances of having brought into her Ladyship's service.

To slip over minutes of no importance to the main of my story, I pass the interval to bedtime in which I was more and more pleased with the views that opened to me of an easy service under these good people, and after supper, being showed up to bed, Miss Phoebe, who observed a kind of modest reluctance in me to strip and go to bed in my shift before her now the maid was withdrawn came up to me, and beginning with unpinning my handkerchief and gown, soon encouraged me to go on with undressing myself, and, still blushing at now seeing myself naked to my shift, I hurried to get under the bedclothes out of sight. Phoebe laughed and was not long before she placed herself by my side. She was about five and twenty, by her own most suspicious account, in which, according to all appearances, she must have sunk at least ten good years, allowance too being made for the havoc which a long course of hackneyship and hot waters must have made of her constitution and which had already brought on, upon the spur, that stale stage in which those of her profession are reduced to think of *showing* company instead of *seeing* it.

No sooner then was this precious substitute of my mistress's lain down, but she, who was never out of her way when any occasion of lewdness presented itself, turned to me, embraced and kissed me with great eagerness. This was new, this was odd; but imputing it to nothing but pure kindness, which, for aught I knew, it might be the London way to express in that manner, I was determined not to be behind-hand with her and returned her the kiss and embrace with all the fervour that perfect innocence knew.

Encouraged by this, her hands became extremely free and wandered over my whole body, with touches, squeezes, pressures that rather warmed and surprised me with their novelty than they either shocked or alarmed me.

The flattering praises she intermingled with these invasions contributed also not a little to bribe my passiveness and knowing no ill, I feared none especially from one who had prevented all doubt of her womanhood by conducting my hands to a pair of breasts that hung loosely down, in a size and volume that full sufficiently distinguished her sex, to me at least who had never made any other comparison.

I lay then all tame and passive as she could wish, whilst her freedom raised no other emotion but those of a strange, and till then unfelt, pleasure: every part of me was open and exposed to the licentious courses of her hands which, like a lambent fire, ran over my whole body and thawed all coldness as they went.

My breasts, if it is not too bold a figure to call so two hard, firm, rising

Gustave Courbet: The Sleepers

hillocks that just began to show themselves or signify anything to the touch, employed and amused her hands awhile, till slipping down lower over a smooth track, she could just feel the soft silky down that had but a few months before put forth and garnished the mount-pleasant of those parts and promised to spread a grateful shelter over the sweet seat of the most exquisite sensation, and which had been, till that instant, the seat of the most insensible innocence. Her fingers played and strove to twine in the young tendrils of that moss which nature has contrived at once for use and ornament.

But not contented with these outer posts, she now attempts the main spot, and began to twitch, to insinuate, and at length to force an introduction of a finger into the quick itself, in such a manner that, had she not proceeded by insensible graduations that enflamed me beyond the power of modesty to oppose its resistence to their progress, I should have jumped out of bed and cried out for help against such strange assaults.

Instead of which, her lascivious touches had lighted up a new fire that wantoned through all my veins but fixed with violence in that center appointed them by nature where the first strange hands were now busied in feeling, squeezing, compressing the lips, then opening them again with a finger between, till an 'Oh!' expressed her hurting me where the narrowness of the unbroken passage refused it entrance to any depth.

In the meantime the extension of my limbs, languid stretchings, sighs, short heavings, all conspired to assure that experienced wanton that I was more pleased than offended at her proceedings, which she seasoned with repeated kisses and exclamations, such as 'Oh! what a charming creature thou art! – What a happy man will he be that first makes a woman of you! – Oh! that I were a man for your sake –!' with the like broken expressions, interrupted by kisses as fierce and salacious as ever I received from the other sex.

For my part, I was transported, confused, and out of myself. Feelings so new were too much for me; my heated and alarmed senses were in a tumult that robbed me of all liberty of thought; tears of pleasure gushed from my eyes and somewhat assuaged the fire that raged all over me.

Phoebe herself, the hackeneyed, thoroughbred Phoebe, to whom all modes and devices of pleasure were known and familiar, found, it seems, in this exercise of her art to break young girls the gratification of one of those arbitrary tastes for which there is no accounting. Not that she hated men or did not even prefer them to her own sex; but when she met with such occasions as this was, a satiety of enjoyments in the common road, perhaps to a secret bias, inclined her to make the most of pleasure wherever she could find it, without distinction of sexes. In this view, now well assured that she had, by her touches, sufficiently inflamed me for her purpose, she rolled down the bedclothes gently, and I saw myself stretched naked, my shift being turned up to my neck, whilst I had no power or sense to oppose it; even my glowing blushes expressed more desire than modesty, whilst the candle left, to be sure not undesignedly, burning, threw a full light on my whole body.

'No! (says Phoebe) you must not, my sweet girl, think to hide all these treasures from me, my sight must be feasted as well as my touch – I must devour with my eyes this springing bosom, – Suffer me to kiss it – I have not seen it enough – Let me kiss it once more – What firm, smooth, white flesh is here – How delicately shaped! – Then this delicious down! Oh! let me view the small, dear, tender cleft! – This is too much, I cannot bear it, I must, I must – ' Here she took my hand and in a transport carried it where you will easily guess; but what a difference in the state of the same thing! – A spreading thicket of bushy curls marked the full-grown complete woman. Then the cavity to which she guided my hand easily received it; and as soon as she felt it within her, she moved herself to and fro, with so rapid a friction that I presently withdrew it, wet and clammy, when instantly Phoebe grew more composed, after two or three sighs, and heart-fetched Oh's! and giving me a kiss that seemed to exhale her soul through her lips, she replaced the bedclothes over us.

What pleasure she had found I will not say; but this I know, that the first sparks of kindling nature, the first ideas of pollution, were caught by me that night, and that the acquaintance and communication with the bad of our own sex is often as fatal to innocence as all the seductions of the other. But to go on: – when Phoebe was restored to that calm which I was far from the enjoyment of myself, she artfully sounded me on all the points necessary to govern the designs of my virtuous mistress on me, and by my answers, drawn from pure undissembled nature, she had no reason but to promise herself all imaginable success, so far as it depended on my ignorance, easiness, and warmth of constitution.

After a sufficient length of dialogue, my bedfellow left me to my rest, and I fell asleep through pure weariness from the violent emotions I had been led into, when nature (which had been too warmly stirred and fermented to subside without allaying by some means or other) relieved me by one of those luscious dreams, the transports of which are scarce inferior to those of waking, real action.

In the morning I awoke about ten, perfectly gay and refreshed; Phoebe was up before me and asked me in the kindest manner how I did, how I had rested, and if I was ready for breakfast, carefully at the same time avoiding to increase the confusion she saw I was in, at looking her in the face, by any hint of the night's bed scene. – I told her if she pleased I would get up and begin any work she would be pleased to set me about. She smiled; presently the maid brought in the tea equippage, and I just huddled my clothes on, when in waddled my mistress. I expected no less than to be told off, if not chid for, my late rising, when I was agreeably disappointed by her compliments on my pure and fresh looks. I was 'a bud of beauty' (this was her style) and how vastly all the fine men would admire me! to all which my answers did not, I can assure you, wrong my breeding: they were as simple and silly as they could wish, and, no doubt, flattered them infinitely more than they had proved me enlightened by education and knowledge of the world.

We breakfasted; and the tea things were scarce removed, when in were brought two bundles of linen and wearing apparel; in short, all the necessaries for *rigging me out*, as they termed it, completely.

Imagine to yourself, Madam, how my little coquette-heart fluttered with joy at the sight of a white lutestring, flowered with silver, scoured indeed, but passed on me for spick and span new, a Brussels lace cap, braided shoes, and the rest in proportion, all second-hand finery, and procured instantly for the occasion by the diligence and industry of the good Mrs Brown, who had already a chapman for me in the house before whom my charms were to pass in review; for he had not only in course insisted on a previous sight of the premises, but also on immediate surrender to him, in case of his agreeing for me; concluding very wisely that such a place as I was in was of the hottest to trust the keeping of such a perishable commodity in as a maidenhead.

The care of dressing and tricking me out for the market was then left to Phoebe, who acquitted herself, if not well, at least perfectly to the satisfaction of everything by my impatience of seeing myself dressed. When it was over, and I viewed myself in the glass, I was, no doubt, too natural, too artless, to hide my childish joy at the change; a change in real truth for much the worse, since I must have much better become the neat easy simplicity of my rustic dress than the awkward, untoward, tawdry finery that I could not conceal my

François Boucher: The Modiste

strangeness to.

Phoebe's compliments, however, in which her own share in dressing me was not forgot, did not a little confirm me in now the first notions I had ever entertained concerning my person, which, be it said without vanity, was then tolerable enough to justify a taste for me, and of which it may not be out of place here to sketch you an unflattered picture.

I was tall, yet not too tall for my age, which, as I before remarked, was barely turned of fifteen, my shape perfectly straight, thin waisted, and light and free, without owing anything to stays. My hair was a glossy auburn and as soft as silk, flowing down my neck in natural buckles, and did not a little set off the whiteness of a smooth skin. My face was rather too ruddy, though its features were delicate, and the shape was a roundish oval, except where a pit in my chin had far from a disagreeable effect; my eyes were as black as can be imagined and rather languishing than sparkling, except on certain occasions, when I have been told they struck fire fast enough; my teeth, which I ever carefully preserved, were small, even, and white; my bosom was finely raised, and one might then discern rather the promise than the actual growth of the round, firm breasts that in a little time made that promise good. In short, all the points of beauty that are most universally in request I had, or at least my vanity forbade me to appeal from the decision of our sovereign judges the men, who all that I ever knew at least gave it thus highly in my favour; and I met with, even in my own sex, some that were above denying me that justice, whilst others praised me yet more unsuspectedly by endeavouring to detract from me in points of person and figure that I obviously excelled in. – This is I own, too much, too strong of self-praise, but should I not be ungrateful to nature, and to a form to which I owe such singular blessings of pleasure and fortune, were I to suppress, through an affectation of modesty, the mention of such valuable gifts?

Well then, dressed I was, and little did it then enter into my head that all this gay attire was no more than decking the victim out for sacrifice, whilst I innocently attributed all to sheer friendship and kindness in the sweet good Mrs Brown who I was forgetting to mention, had, under pretence of keeping my money safe, got from me, without the least hesitation, the driblet (so I now call it) which remained to me after the expenses of my journey.

After some little time, most agreeably spent before the glass in scarce self-admiration, since my new dress had by much the greatest share in it, I was sent for down to the parlour where the old lady saluted me, and wished me joy of my new clothes, which, she was not ashamed to say, fitted me as if I had worn nothing but the finest all my lifetime; but what was it she could not see me silly enough to swallow? At the same time she presented me to another cousin of her own creation, an elderly gentleman, who got up at my entry into the room, and on my dropping a curtsy to him, saluted me and seemed a little affronted that I had only presented my cheek to him, a mistake which, if one, he immediately corrected by glueing his lips to mine with an ardour which his figure had not at all disposed me to thank him for: his figure, I say, than which nothing could be more shocking or detestable; for ugly and disagreeable were terms too gentle to convey a just idea of it.

Imagine to yourself a man rather past threescore, short and ill made, with a yellow cadaverous hue, great goggling eyes that stared as if he was strangled; an out-mouth from two more properly tushes than teeth, livid lips, and a breath like a jakes. Then he had a peculiar ghastliness in his grin that made him perfectly frightful, if not dangerous to women with child; yet, made as he was thus in mock of man, he was so blind to his own staring deformities as to think himself born for pleasing, and that no woman could see him with impunity; in consequence of which idea he had lavished great sums on such wretches as could gain upon themselves to pretend love to his person, whilst to those who had not art or patience to dissemble the horror it inspired he behaved even brutally. Impotence, more than necessity, made him seek in variety the provocative that was wanting to raise him to the pitch of enjoyment, which too he often saw himself balked of by the failure of his powers: and this always threw him into a fit of rage, which he wreaked, as far as he durst, on the innocent objects of his fit of momentary desire.

This then was the monster to which my conscientious benefactress, who had long been his purveyor in this way, had doomed me, and sent for me down purposely for this examination. Accordingly, she made me stand up before him, turned me round, unpinned my handkerchief, remarked to him the rise and fall, the turn and whiteness of a bosom just beginning to fill; then made me walk, and took even a handle from the rusticity of my gait to inflame the inventory of my charms. In short, she omitted no point of jockeyship, to which he only answered by gracious nods of approbation whilst he looked goats and monkeys at me: for I sometimes stole a corner-glance at him, and, encountering his fiery eager stare, looked another way from pure horror and affright, which he, doubtless in character, attributed to nothing more than maiden modesty, or at least the affectation of it.

Thomas Rowlandson: The Fumbler

However, I was soon dismissed and reconducted to my room by Phoebe, who stuck close to me, by way of not leaving me alone and at leisure, to make such reflections as might naturally rise to anyone not an idiot on such a scene as I had just gone through; but to my shame be it confessed that such was my invincible stupidity, or rather portentous innocence, that I did not yet open my eyes on Mrs Brown's designs, and saw nothing in this titular cousin of her's but a shocking hideous person, which did not at all concern me, unless that my gratitude for my benefactress made me extend my respect to all her cousinhood.

Phoebe, however, began to sift the state and pulses of my heart towards this monster, asking me how I should approve of such a fine gentleman for a husband? (fine gentleman, I suppose she called him, from his being daubed with lace). I answered her very naturally that I had no thoughts of a husband, but that if I was to choose one, it should be among my own degree sure! So much had my aversion to that wretch's hideous figure indisposed me to all *fine gentlemen* and confounded my ideas, as if those of that rank had been necessarily cast in the same mould that he was. But Phoebe was not to be beat off so, but went on with her endeavours to melt and soften me for the purposes of my reception into that hospitable house; and whilst she talked of the sex in general, she had no reason to despair of a compliance, which more than one reason showed her would be easily enough obtained of me. But then she had too much experience not to discover that my particular fixed aversion to that frightful cousin would be a block not so readily to be removed as suited with the consummation of their bargain and sale of me.

Mother Brown had in the meantime agreed the terms with this liquorish old goat, which I afterwards understood were to be fifty guineas peremptory for the liberty of attempting me, and a hundred more at the complete gratification of his desires in the triumph over my virginity; and as for me, I was to be left entirely at the discretion of his liking and generosity. This unrighteous contract being thus settled, he was so eager to be put in possession that he insisted on being introduced to drink tea with me that afternoon, when we were to be left alone; nor would he hearken to the procuress's remonstrances that I was not sufficiently prepared and ripened for such an attack, that I was yet too green and untamed, having been scarce twenty-four hours in her house; it is the character of lust to be impatient, and his vanity arming him against any supposition of other than the common resistance of a maid on those occasions, made him reject all proposals of delay, and my dreadful trial was thus fixed, unknown to me, that very evening.

At dinner, Mrs Brown and Phoebe did nothing but run riot in praises of this wonderful cousin, and how happy that woman would be that he would favour with his addresses. In short, my two gossips exhausted all their rhetoric to persuade me to accept them: that the gentleman was violently smitten with me at first sight . . . that he would make my fortune if I would be a good girl and not stand in my own light . . . that I should trust his honour . . . that I should be made for ever and have a chariot to go abroad in . . . with all such stuff as was fit to turn the head of such silly ignorant girl as I then was. But luckily here my aversion had taken already such deep root in me, my heart was so strongly defended from him by my senses that, wanting the art to mask my sentiments, I gave them no hopes of their employer's succeeding, at least very easily, with me. The glass too marched pretty quick, with a view, I suppose, to make a friend of the warmth of my constitution in the minutes of the imminent attack.

Thus they kept me pretty long at table, and about six in the evening, after I was retired to my own apartment and the tea-board was set, enters my venerable mistress, followed close by that satyr, who came in grinning in a way peculiar to him, and by his odious presence confirmed me in all the sentiments of detestation which his first appearance had given birth to.

He sat down fronting me, and all teatime kept ogling me in a manner that gave me the utmost pain and confusion, all the marks of which he still explained to be my bashfulness and not being used to see company.

Tea over, the commode old lady pleaded urgent business (which indeed was true) to go out, and earnestly desired me to entertain her cousin *kindly* till she came back, both for my own sake and her's; and then, with a 'Pray, sir, be very good, be very tender of the sweet child,' she went out of the room leaving me staring, with my mouth open and unprepared, by the suddenness of her departure, to oppose it.

We were now alone: and on that idea a sudden fit of trembling seized me; – I was so afraid, without a precise notion of why and what I had to fear, that I sat on the settee by the fireside, motionless and petrified, without life or spirit, not knowing how to look or how to stir.

But long I was not suffered to remain in this state of stupefaction: the monster squatted down by me on the settee, and without farther ceremony, or preamble, flings his arms about my neck, and drawing me pretty forcibly towards him, obliged me to receive, in spite of my struggles to disengage from him, his pestilential kisses, which quite overcame me. Finding me then next to senseless and unresisting, he tears off my neck handkechief and laid all open there to his eyes and hands; still I endured all without flinching, till emboldened by my sufferance and silence (for I had not the power to speak or cry out), he attempted to lay me down on the settee, and I felt his hand on the lower part of my naked thighs, which were crossed and which he endeavoured to unlock. Oh then! I was roused out of my passive endurance, and springing from him with an activity he was not prepared for, threw myself at his feet and begged him, in the most moving tone, not to be rude, and that he would not hurt me: 'Hurt you, my dear!' says the brute, 'I intend you no harm . . . has not the old lady told you that I loved you? . . . that I shall do handsomely by you?' 'She has indeed, sir,' said I, 'but I cannot love you, indeed I cannot! – pray, let me alone . . . yes! I will love you dearly if you will let me alone, and go away . . . ' But I was talking to the wind: for whether my tears, my attitude, or the disorder of my dress proved fresh incentives, or whether he was now under the dominion of desires he could not bridle, but snorting and foaming with lust and rage, he renews his attack, seizes me, and again attempts to extend and fix me on the settee; in which he succeeded so far as to lay me along and even to toss my petticoats over my head, and lay my thighs bare, which I obstinately kept close, nor could he, though he attempted with his knee to force them open, effect it so as to stand fair for being master of the main avenue. He was unbuttoned, both waistcoat and breeches, yet I only felt the weight of his body upon me, whilst I lay struggling with indignation, and dying with terrors; but he stopped all of a sudden, and got off, panting, blowing, cursing, and rehearsing upon me *old* and *ugly!* for so I had very naturally called him in the heat of my defence.

The brute had, it seems, as I afterwards understood, brought on, by his eagerness and struggle, the ultimate period of his hot fit of lust, which his power was too short-lived to carry him through the full execution of; of which my thighs and linen received the effusion.

When it was over he bid me, with a tone of displeasure, get up . . . that he would not do me the honour to think of me any more . . . that the old b – h might look out for another cully . . . that he would not be fooled so by ever a country mock modesty in England . . . that he supposed I had left my maidenhead with some hobnail in the country, and was come to dispose of my skim-milk in town, with a volley of the like abuse which I listened to with more pleasure than ever fond woman did to protestations of love from her

Thomas Rowlandson: Death Helping an Old Lover into Bed

darling minion: for, uncapable as I was of receiving any addition to my perfect hatred and aversion to him, I looked on his railing as my security against his renewing his most odious caresses.

Yet, plain as Mrs Brown's views were now come out, I had not the heart or spirit to open my eyes on them. Still I could not part with my dependence on that beldam; so much did I think myself her's, soul and body; or rather, I sought to deceive myself with the continuation of my good opinion of her, and chose to wait the worst at her hands, sooner than being turned out to starve in the streets, without a penny of money or a friend to apply to: these fears were my folly.

Whilst this confusion of ideas was passing in my head, and I sat pensive by the fire, with my eyes brimming with tears, my neck still bare, and my cap fallen off in the struggle, so that my hair was in the disorder you may guess, the villain's lust began, I suppose, to be again in flow, at the sight of all that bloom of youth which presented itself to his view, a bloom yet unenjoyed and in course not yet indifferent to him.

After some pause, he asked me, with a tone of voice mightily softened, whether I would make it up with him before the old lady returned, and all should be well; he would restore me his affections, at the same time offering to kiss me and feel my breasts. But now my extreme aversion, my fears, my indignation, all acting upon me, gave me a spirit not natural to me, so that breaking loose from him, I ran to the bell and rang it before he was aware, with such violence and effect as brought up the maid to know what was the matter, or whether the gentleman wanted anything? And before he could proceed to greater extremities, she bounced into the room, and seeing me stretched on the floor, my hair all dishevelled, my nose gushing out blood (which did not a little tragedize the scene) and my odious persecutor still intent on pushing his brutal point, unmoved by all my cries and distress, she was herself confounded and did not know what to do.

As much, however, as Martha might be prepared and hardened to transactions of this sort, all womanhood must have been out of her heart, could she have seen this unmoved. Besides that, on the face of things she imagined that matters had gone greater lengths than they really had, and that the courtesy of the house had been actually consummated on me and flung me into the condition I was in: in this notion she instantly took my part and advised the gentleman to go down and leave me to recover myself, and that all would be soon over with me – that when Mrs Brown and Phoebe, who were gone out, were returned, they would take order for everything to his satisfaction – that nothing would be lost by a little patience with the poor tender thing – that for her part, she was frightened – she could not tell what to say to such doings – but that she would stay by me till my mistress came home. As the wench said all this in a resolute tone, and the monster himself began to perceive that things would not mend by his staying, he took his hat and went out of the room murmuring and pleating his brows like an old ape, so that I was delivered from the horrors of his detestable presence.

As soon as he was gone, Martha very tenderly offered me her assistance in anything, and would have got me some hartshorn drops and put me to bed; which last I at first positively refused, in the fear that the monster might return and take me at that advantage. However, with much persuasion and assurances that I should not be molested that night, she prevailed on me to lie down; and indeed I was so weakened by my struggles, so dejected by my fearful apprehensions, so terror-struck, that I had no power to sit up or hardly to give answers to the questions with which the curious Martha plied and perplexed me.

Such, too, and so cruel was my fate that I dreaded the sight of Mrs Brown, as if I had been the criminal and she the person injured, a mistake which you will not think so strange on distinguishing that neither virtue or principles had the least share in the defence I had made but only the particular aversion I had conceived against this first brutal and frightful invader of my tender innocence.

I passed then the time till Mrs Brown's return home, under all the agitations of fear and despair that may easily be guessed.

About eleven at night my two ladies came home, and having received rather a favourable account from Martha, who had run down to let them in (for Mr Crofts, that was the name of my brute, was gone out of the house, after waiting till he had tired his patience for Mrs Brown's return), they came thundering upstairs, and seeing me pale, my face bloody, and all the marks of the most thorough dejection, they employed themselves more to comfort and re-inspirit me than in making me the reproaches I was weak enough to fear, I who had so many juster and stronger to retort upon them.

Mrs Brown withdrawn, Phoebe came presently to bed to me, and what with the answers she drew from me, what with her own method of *palpably* satisfying herself, she soon discovered that I had been more frightened than hurt; upon which, I suppose being herself seized with sleep and reserving her lectures and instructions till the next morning, she left me, properly speaking, to my unrest: for after tossing and turning the greatest part of the night, and tormenting myself with the falsest notions and apprehensions of things, I fell, through mere fatigue, into a kind of delirious doze, out of which I waked late in the morning in a violent fever; a circumstance which was extremely critical to reprieve me, at least for a time, from the attacks of a wretch infinitely more terrible to me than death itself.

The interested care that was taken of me during my illness, in order to restore me to a condition of making good the bawd's engagements or of enduring further trials, had, however, such an effect on my grateful disposition that I even thought myself obliged to my undoers for their attentions to promote my recovery, and, above all, for the keeping out of my sight that brutal ravisher, the author of my disorder, on their finding I was too strongly moved at the bare mention of his name.

Youth is soon raised; and a few days were sufficient to conquer the fury of my fever; but what contributed most to my perfect recovery and to my reconciliation with life was the timely news that Mr Crofts, who was a merchant of considerable dealings, was arrested at the king's suit, for near forty thousand pounds, on account of his driving a certain contraband trade, and that his affairs were so desperate that even were it in his inclination, it would not be in his power to renew his designs upon me: for he was instantly thrown into a prison, which it was not likely that he would get out of in haste.

Mrs Brown, who had touched his fifty guineas, advanced to so little purpose, and lost all hopes of the remaining hundred, began to look upon my treatment of him with a more favourable eye; and as they had observed my temper to be perfectly tractable and conformable to their views, all the girls that composed her flock were suffered to visit me and had their cue to dispose me, by their conversation, to a perfect resignation of myself to Mrs Brown's direction.

Accordingly they were let in upon me, and all that frolic and thoughtless gaiety in which those giddy creatures consume their leisure made me envy a condition of which I only saw the fair side; insomuch that the being one of them became even my ambition: a disposition which they all carefully cultivated; and I wanted now nothing but to restore my health, that I might be able to undergo the ceremony of the initiation.

Conversation, example, all, in short, contributed in that house to corrupt my native purity, which had taken no root in education, whilst now the inflammable principle of pleasure, so easily fired at my age, made strange work within me, and all the modesty I was brought up in the habit (not the instruction) of, began to melt away, like dew before the sun's heat; not to mention that I made a vice of necessity, from the constant fears I had of being turned out to starve.

I was soon pretty well recovered, and at certain hours allowed to range all over the house, but cautiously kept from seeing any company, till the arrival of Lord B – from Bath, to whom Mrs Brown, in respect to his experienced generosity on such occasions, proposed to offer the refusal of that trinket of mine, which bears so great an imaginary value: and his lordship being expected in town in less than a fortnight, Mrs Brown judged I should be entirely renewed in beauty and freshness by that time and afford her the chance of a better bargain than she had driven with Mr Crofts.

In the meantime, I was so thoroughly, as they call it, brought over, so tame to their whistle, that, had my cage door been set open, I had no idea that I ought to fly anywhere sooner than stay where I was; nor had I the least sense of regretting my condition, but waited very quietly for whatever Mrs Brown should order concerning me, who on her side, by herself and her agents, took more than the necessary precautions to lull and lay asleep all just reflections on my destination.

Preachments of morality over the left shoulder, a life of joy painted in the gayest colours, caresses, promises, indulgent treatment; nothing, in short, was wanting to domesticate me entirely and to prevent my going out anywhere to get better advice; alas! I dreamed of no such thing.

Hitherto I had been indebted only to the girls of the house for the corruption of my innocence; their luscious talk, in which modesty was far from respected, their descriptions of their engagements with men, had given me a tolerable insight into the nature and mysteries of their profession, at the same time that they highly provoked an itch of florid warm-spirited blood through every vein; but above all, my bedfellow, Phoebe, whose pupil I more immediately was, exerted her talents in giving me the first tinctures of pleasure: whilst nature now warmed and wantoned with discoveries so interesting, piqued a curiosity which Phoebe artfully whetted, and leading me from question to question of her own suggestion, explained to me all the mysteries of Venus. But I could not long remain in such a house as that, without being an eye-witness of more than I could conceive from her descriptions.

One day about twelve at noon, being thoroughly recovered of my fever, I happened to be in Mrs Brown's dark closet, where I had not been half an hour, resting on the maid's settle-bed, before I heard a rustling in the bed-chamber, separated from the closet only by two sash-doors, before the glasses of which were drawn two yellow damask curtains, but not so close as to exclude the full view of the room from any person in the closet.

I instantly crept softly, and posted myself so that, seeing everything minutely, I could not myself be seen; and who should come in but the venerable mother abbess herself! handed in by a tall, brawny, young horse-grenadier, moulded in the Hercules-style; in fine, the choice of the most experienced dame, in those affairs, in all London.

Oh! how still and hush did I keep at my stand, lest any noise should balk my curiosity, or bring madam into the closet!

But I had not much reason to fear either, for she was so entirely taken up with her present great concern that she had no sense of attention to spare to anything else.

Droll was it to see that clumsy fat figure of her's flop down on the foot of the bed, opposite to the closet door, so that I had a full front view of all her charms.

Her paramour sat down by her. He seemed to be a man of very few words, and a great stomach, for proceeding instantly to essentials, he gave her some hearty smacks, and thrusting his hands into her breasts, disengaged them from her stays, in scorn of whose confinement they broke loose and swagged down, navel low at least. A more enormous pair did my eyes never behold, nor of a worse colour, flagging soft, and most lovingly contiguous: yet such as they were, this neck-beef-eater seemed to paw them with a most unenviable gust, seeking in vain to confine or cover one of them with a hand scarce less than a shoulder of mutton. After toying with them thus some time, as if they had been worth it, he laid her down pretty briskly, and canting up her petticoats, made barely a mask of them to her broad red face, that blushed with nothing but brandy.

As he stood on one side for a minute or so, unbuttoning his waistcoat and breeches, her fat brawny thighs hung down; and the whole greasy landscape lay fairly open to my view: a wide open-mouthed gap, over-shaded with a grizzly bush seemed held out like a beggar's wallet for its provision.

But I soon had my eyes called off by a more striking object, that entirely engrossed them.

Her sturdy stallion had now unbuttoned, and produced naked, stiff, and erect, that wonderful machine, which I had never seen before, and which, for the interest my own seat of pleasure began to take furiously in it, I stared at with all the eyes I had. However, my senses were too much flurried, too much concentered in that now burning spot of mine, to observe anything more than in general the make and turn of that instrument, from which the instinct of nature, yet more than all I had heard of it, now strongly informed me I was to expect that supreme pleasure which she has placed in the meeting of those parts so admirably fitted for each other.

de St Aubin: Be Discreet

Long, however, the young spark did not remain, before, giving it two or three shakes, by way of brandishing it, he threw himself upon her, and his back being now towards me, I could only take his being engulfed for granted, by the direction he moved in, and the impossibility of missing so staring a mark; and now the bed shook, the curtains rattled so, that I could scarce hear the sighs and murmurs, the heaves and pantings that accompanied the action, from the beginning to the end; the sound and sight of which thrilled to the very soul of me, and made every vein of my body circulate liquid fires: the emotion grew so violent that it almost intercepted my respiration.

Prepared then, and disposed as I was by the discourse of my companions, and Phoebe's minute detail of everything, no wonder that such a sight gave the last dying blow to my native innocence.

Whilst they were in the heat of the action, guided by nature only, I stole my hand up my petticoat, and with fingers all on fire, seized and yet more inflamed that center of all my senses; my heart palpitated, as if it would force its way through my bosom; I breathed with pain; I twisted my thighs, squeezed and compressed the lips of that virgin slit, and following mechanically the example of Phoebe's manual operation on it, as far as I could find admission, brought on at last the critical ecstasy, the melting flow, into which nature, spent with excess of pleasure, dissolves and dies away.

After which my senses recovered coolness enough to observe the rest of the transaction between this happy pair.

The young fellow had just dismounted, when the old lady immediately sprang up, with all the vigour of youth, derived no doubt from her late refreshment, and making him sit down, began in her turn to kiss him, to pat and pinch his cheeks, and play with his hair, all which he received with an air of indifference and coolness that showed him to me much altered from what he was when he first went on to the breach.

My pious governess, however, not being above calling in auxiliaries, unlocks a little case of cordials that stood near the bed, and made him pledge her in a very plentiful dram; after which and a little amorous parley, madam sat herself down upon the same place at the bed's foot; and the young fellow standing sideways by her, she, with the greatest effrontery imaginable, unbuttons his breeches, and removing his shirt, draws out his affair, so shrunk and diminished that I could not but remember the difference, now crestfallen, or just faintly lifting its head. But our experienced matron very soon, by chafing it with her hands, brought it to swell to that size and erection I had before seen it up to.

I admired then, upon a fresh account, and with a nicer survey, the texture of that capital part of man: the flaming red head as it stood uncapped, the whiteness of the shaft, and the shrub-growth of curling hair that embrowned the roots of it, the roundish bag that dangled down from it, all exacted my eager attention and renewed my flame; but as the main affair was now at the point the industrious dame had laboured to bring it to, she was not in the humour to put off the payment of her pains, but laying herself down, drew him gently upon her, and thus they finished, in the same manner as before, the old last act.

This over, they both went out lovingly together, the old lady having first

Joseph Highmore: Pamela in the Bedroom with Mrs Jewkes (*detail*)

made him a present, as near as I could observe, of three or four pieces; he being not only her particular favourite on the account of his performances, but a retainer to the house, from whose sight she had taken great care hither to secrete me, lest he might not have had patience to wait for my lord's arrival, but have insisted on being his taster, which the old lady was under too much subjection to him to dare dispute with him; for every girl of the house fell to him in course, and the old lady only now and then got her turn, in consideration of the maintenance he had, and which he could scarce be accused of not earning from her.

As soon as I heard them go downstairs, I stole up softly to my own room, out of which I had been luckily not missed. There I began to breathe a little freer, and to give a loose to those warm emotions which the sight of such an encounter had raised in me. I laid me down on the bed, stretched myself out, joining, and ardently wishing, and requiring any means to divert or allay the rekindled rage and tumult of my desires, which all pointed strongly to their pole, man. I felt about the bed, as if I sought for something that I grasped in my waking dream, and not finding it, could have cried for vexation, every part of me glowing with stimulating fires. At length, I resorted to the only present remedy, that of vain attempts at digitation, where the smallness of the theater did not yet afford room enough for action, where the pain my fingers gave me in striving for admission, though they procured me a slight satisfaction for the present, started an apprehension, which I could not be easy till I had communicated to Phoebe and received her explanations upon it.

The opportunity, however, did not offer till next morning, for Phoebe did not come to bed till long after I was gone to sleep. As soon then as we were both awake, it was but in course to bring our lie-a-bed chat to land on the subject of my uneasiness, to which a recital of the love-scene I had thus by a chance been spectatress of, served for a preface.

Phoebe could not hear it to the end without more than one interruption by peals of laughter, and my ingenuous way of relating matters did not a little heighten the joke to her.

But on her sounding me how the sight had affected me, without mincing or hiding the pleasurable emotions it had inspired me with, I told her at the same time that one remark had perplexed me, and that very considerably: 'Ay!' says she, 'what was that?' 'Why,' replied I, having very curiously and attentively compared the size of that enormous machine, which did not appear, at least to my fearful imagination, less than my wrist, and at least three of my handfuls long, to that of the tender, small part of me which was framed to receive it, I could not conceive its being possible to afford it entrance without dying, perhaps in the greatest pain, since she well knew that even a finger thrust in there, hurt me beyond bearing . . . 'As to my mistress's and your's . . . I can very plainly distinguish the different dimensions of them from mine, palpable to the touch, and visible to the eye, so that in short, great as the promised pleasure may be, I am afraid of the pain of the experiment.'

Phoebe at this redoubled her laugh, and, whilst I expected a very serious solution of my doubts and apprehensions in this matter, only told me that she never heard of a mortal wound being given, in those parts, by that terrible weapon, and that some she knew younger and as delicately made as myself, had outlived the operation, that she believed, at the worst, I would take a great deal of killing . . . that true it was, there was a great diversity of sizes in those parts, owing to nature, child-bearing, frequent over-stretching with unmerciful machines; but that at a certain age and habit of body, even the most experienced in those affairs could not well distinguish between the maid and the woman, supposing too an absence of all artifice, and things in their natural sitation; but that since chance had thrown in my way one sight of that sort, she would procure me another, that should feast my eyes more delicately, and go a great way in the cure of my fears from that imaginary disproportion.

On this she asked me if I knew Polly Philips. 'Undoubtedly,' says I, 'the fair girl which was so tender of me when I was sick, and has been, as you told me, but two months in the house?' 'The same,' says Phoebe. 'You must know then, she is kept by a young Genoese merchant, whom his uncle, who is immensely rich and whose darling he is, sent over here with an English merchant, his friend, on a pretext of settling some accounts, but in reality to humour his inclinations for travelling and seeing the world. He met casually with this Polly once in company and taking a liking to her, makes it worth her while to keep entirely to him. He comes to her here twice or thrice a week, and she receives him in the light closet up one pair of stairs, where he enjoys her in a taste I suppose peculiar to the heat, or perhaps the caprices of his own country. I say no more; but tomorrow being his day, you shall see what passes between them, from a place only known to your mistress and myself.'

You may be sure, in the ply I was now taking, I had no objection to the proposal and was rather a-tiptoe for its accomplishment.

At five in the evening then, next day, Phoebe, punctual to her promise, came to me as I sat alone in my own room, and beckoned me to follow her.

We went down the backstairs very softly, and opening the door of a dark closet, where there was some old furniture kept and some cases of liquors, she drew me in after her, and fastening the door upon us, we had no light but what came through a long crevice in the partition between ours and the light closet, where the scene of action lay; so that sitting on those low cases, we could, with the greatest ease as well as clearness, see all objects (ourselves unseen) only by applying our eyes close to the crevice, where the moulding of a panel had warped or started a little on the other side.

The young gentleman was the first person I saw, with his back directly towards me, looking at a print. Polly was not yet come. In less than a minute though, the door opened, and she came in, and at the noise the door made, he turned about, and came to meet her, with an air of the greatest tenderness and satisfaction.

After saluting her, he led her to a couch that fronted us, where they both sat down, and the young Genoese helped her to a glass of wine, with some Naples biscuit on a salver.

Presently, when they had exchanged a few kisses, and questions in broken English on one side, he began to unbutton, and, in fine, stripped into his shirt.

As if this had been the signal agreed on for pulling off all their clothes, a scheme which the heat of the season perfectly favoured, Polly began to draw her pins, and as she had no stays to unlace she was in a trice, with her gallant's officious assistance, undressed to all but her shift.

When he saw this, his breeches were immediately loosened, waist and knee-bands, and slipped over his ankles, clean off; his shirt collar was unbuttoned too. Then first giving Polly an encouraging kiss, he stole as it were the shift off the girl, who, being I suppose broke and familiarized to this humour, blushed indeed, but less than I did, at the apparition of her now standing stark-naked, just as she came out of the hands of pure nature, with her black hair loose, and a-float down her dazzling white neck and shoulders, whilst the deepened carnation of her cheeks went off gradually into the hue of glazed snow; for such were the blended tints and polish of her skin.

This girl could not be above eighteen. Her face regular and sweet-featured, her shape exquisite; nor could I help envying her two ripe enchanting breasts, finely plumped out in flesh, but withal so round, so firm, that they sustained themselves, in scorn of any stay. Then their nipples pointing different ways

Thomas Rowlandson: The Willing Fair

marked their pleasing separation; beneath them lay the delicious tract of the belly, which terminated in a parting or rift scarce discernible, that modestly seemed to retire downwards, and seek shelter between two plump fleshy thighs: the curling hair that overspread its delightful front, clothed it with the richest sable fur in the universe. In short, she was evidently a subject for the painters to court her sitting to them for a pattern of female beauty, in all the true pride and pomp of nakedness.

The young Italian (still in his shirt) stood gazing and transported at the sight of beauties that might have fired a dying hermit; his eager eyes devoured her, as she shifted attitudes at his discretion; neither were his hands excluded their share of the high feast, but wandered, on the hunt of pleasure, over every part and inch of her body so qualified to afford the most exquisite sense of it.

In the meantime, one could not help observing the swell of his shirt before, that bolstered out, and pointed out the condition of things behind the curtain. But he soon removed it by slipping his shirt over his head; and now, as to nakedness, they had nothing to reproach one another.

The young gentleman, by Phoebe's guess, was about two and twenty: tall and well limbed. His body was finely formed and of a most vigorous make, square-shouldered, and broad-chested. His face was not remarkable in any way, but for a nose inclining to the Roman, eyes large, black, and sparkling, and a ruddiness in his cheeks that was the more a grace for his complexion being of the brownest, not of that dusky dun colour which excludes the idea of freshness, but of that clear, olive gloss, which, glowing with life, dazzles perhaps less than fairness, and yet pleases more, when it pleases at all. His hair, being too short to tie, fell no lower than his neck, in short easy curls; and he had a few sprigs about his paps, that garnished his chest in a style of strength and manliness. Then his grand movement, which seemed to rise out of a thicket of curling hair that spread from the root all around his thighs and belly up to the navel, stood stiff, and upright, but of a size to frighten me, by sympathy, for the small tender part, which was the object of its fury, and which now lay exposed to my fairest view: for he had immediately, on stripping off his shirt, gently pushed her down on the couch, which stood conveniently to break her willing fall. Her thighs were spread out to their utmost extension, and discovered between them the mark of the sex, the red-centred cleft of flesh, whose lips vermillioning inwards, expressed a small rubied line in sweet miniature, such as not Guido's touch or colouring could ever attain to the life or delicacy of.

Phoebe, at this, gave me a gentle jog to prepare me for a whispered question: whether I thought my little maiden-toy was much less? But my attention was too much engrossed, too much enwrapped with all I saw, to be able to give her any answer.

By this time the young gentleman had changed her posture from lying breadth- to length wise on the couch; but her thighs were still spread, and the mark lay fair for him, who, now kneeling between them, displayed to us a side-view of that fierce erect machine of his, which threatened no less than splitting the tender victim, who lay smiling at the uplifted stroke, nor seemed to decline it. He looked upon his weapon himself with some pleasure, and guiding it with his hand to the inviting slit, drew aside the lips and lodged it (after some thrusts, which Polly seemed even to assist) about half way. But there it stuck, I suppose, from its growing thickness. He draws it again, and just wetting it with spittle, re-enters, and with ease sheathed it now up to the hilt, at which Polly gave a deep sigh, which was quite in another tone than one of pain; he thrusts, she heaves, at first gently, and in a regular cadence, but presently the transport began to be too violent to observe any order or measure, their motions were too rapid, their kisses too fierce and fervent for nature to support such fury long; both seemed to me out of themselves, their eyes darted fires; 'Oh! Oh! – I can't bear it – it is too much – I die – I am a going –' were Polly's expressions of ecstasy. His joys were more silent; but soon broken murmurs, sighs heart-fetched, and at length a dispatching thrust, as if he would have forced himself up her body, and then the motionless languor of all his limbs, all showed that the die-away moment was come upon him, which she gave signs of joining with, by the wild throwing of her hands about, closing her eyes, and giving a deep sob, in which she seemed to expire in an agony of bliss.

When he had finished his stroke and got from off her, she lay still without the least motion, breathless, as it should seem, with pleasure. He replaced her again breadthwise on the couch, unable to sit up, with her thighs open, between which I could observe a kind of white liquid, like froth, hanging about the outward lips of that recent opened wound, which now glowed with a deeper red. Presently she gets up, and throwing her arms round him, seemed far from undelighted with the trial he had put her to, judge at least by the fondness with which she eyed and hung upon him.

For my part, I will not pretend to describe what I felt all over me during this scene; but from that instant, adieu all fears of what man could do unto me; they were now changed into such ardent desires, such ungovernable longings, that I could have pulled the first of that sex that should present himself by the sleeve and offered him the bauble, which I now imagined the loss of would be a gain I could not too soon procure myself.

Phoebe, who had more experience, and to whom such sights were not so new, could not however be unmoved at so warm a scene; and drawing me away softly from the peep-hole, for fear of being overheard, guided me as near the door as possible; all passive and obedient to her least signals.

Here was no room either to sit or lie, but making me stand with my back towards the door, she lifted up my petticoats, and with her busy fingers fell to visit and explore that part of me where now the heat and irritations were so violent that I was perfectly sick and ready to die with desire: that the bare touch of her finger in that critical place had the effect of fire to a train, and her hand instantly made her sensible to what a pitch I was wound up, and melted by the sight she had thus procured me. Satisfied then with her success in allaying a heat that would have made me impatient of seeing the continuation of transactions between our amorous couple, she brought me again to the crevice so favourable to our curiosity.

We had certainly been but a few instants away from it, and yet on our return we saw everything in good forwardness for recommencing the tender hostilities.

The young foreigner was sitting down, fronting us, on the couch; with Polly upon one knee, who had her arms round his neck, whilst the extreme whiteness of her skin was not undelightfully contrasted by the smooth glossy brown of her lover's.

But who could count the fierce unnumbered kisses given and taken in which I could often discover their exchanging the velvet thrust, when both their mouths were double-tongued, and seemed to favour the mutual insertion with the greatest gust and delight.

In the meantime, his red-headed champion, that had so lately fled the pit, quelled and abashed, was now recovered to the top of its condition, perked and crested up between Polly's thighs, who was not wanting on her part to coax and keep it in good humour, stroking it with her head down, and received even its velvet tip between the lips of not its proper mouth; whether she did this out of any particular pleasure, or whether it was to render it more glib and easy of entrance, I could not tell. But it had such an effect that the young gentleman seemed by his eyes, that sparkled with more excited lustre, and his inflamed countenance, to receive increase of pleasure. He got up, and taking Polly in his arms, embraced her and said something too softly for me to hear, leading her withal to the foot of the couch, and taking delight to slap her thighs and posteriors with that stiff sinew of his, which hit them with a spring that he gave it with his hand, and made them resound again, but hurt her about as much as he meant to hurt her, for she seemed to have as frolic a taste as himself.

But guess my surprise, when I saw the lazy young rogue lie down on his back and gently pull down Polly upon him, who giving way to his humour, straddled and with her hands conducted her blind favourite to the right place, and following her impulse, ran directly upon the flaming point of this weapon of pleasure, which she staked herself upon, up-pierced and infixed to the extremest hair-breadth of it: thus she sat on him, a few instants, enjoying and relishing her situation, whilst he toyed with her provoking breasts. -Sometimes she would stoop to meet his kiss; but presently the sting of pleasure spurred them up to fiercer action: then began the storm of heaves, which, from the under-most combatant, were thrusts at the same time, he crossing his hands over her and drawing her home to him with a sweet violence. The inverted strokes of anvil over hammer soon brought on the critical period, in which all the signs of a close conspiring ecstasy informed us of the *point* they were at.

For me, I could bear to see nor more: I was so overcome, so inflamed at this second part of the same play that, mad with intolerable desire, I hugged, I clasped Phoebe, as if she had had wherewithal to relieve me. Pleased, however with, and pitying the taking she could feel me in, she drew me towards the door and opening it as softly as she could, we both got off undiscovered, and she reconducted me to my own room, where unable to keep my legs in the agitation I was in, I instantly threw myself down on the bed, where I lay transported, though ashamed at what I felt.

Phoebe lay down by me and asked me archly if, now that I had seen the enemy and full considered him, I was still afraid of him? Or did I think I could venture to come to a close engagement with him? To all which not a word on my side. I sighed and could scarce breathe. She takes hold of my hand, and having rolled up her own petticoats, forced it half-strivingly towards those parts, where, now grown more knowing, I missed the main object of my wishes; and finding not even the shadow of what I wanted, where everything was so flat! or so hollow! in the vexation I was in at it, I should have withdrawn my hand, but for fear of disobliging her. Abandoning it then entirely to her management, she made use of it as she thought proper, to procure herself rather the shadow than the substance of any pleasure. For my part, I now pined for more solid food, and promised tacitly to myself that I would not be put off much longer with this foolery from woman to woman, if Mrs Brown did not soon provide me with the essential specific: in short, I had all the air of not being able to wait the arrival of my lord B – , though he was now expected in a very few days: nor did I wait for him, for love itself took charge of the disposal of me, in spite of interest, or gross lust.

It was now two days after the closet-scene, that I got up about six in the morning, and leaving my bedfellow fast asleep, stole down, with no other thought than of taking a little fresh air in a small garden, which our back-parlour opened into, and from which my confinement debarred me at the times company came to the house; but now sleep and silence reigned all over it.

I opened the parlour-door, and well surprised was I at seeing, by the side of a fire half out, a young gentleman in the old lady's elbow-chair, with his legs laid upon another, fast asleep, and left there by his thoughtless companions, who had drank him down and then went off with every one his mistress, whilst he stayed behind by the curtesy of the old matron, who would not disturb or turn him out in that condition at one in the morning, and beds, it is more than probable, there were none to spare. On the table still remained the punch-bowl and glasses, strewed about in their usual disorder after a drunken revel.

But when I drew nearer to view the sleeping estray, heavens! what a sight! no! no terms of years, no turns of fortune could ever erase the lightning-like impression his form made on me . . . Yes! dearest object of my earliest passion, I command for ever the remembrance of thy first appearance to my ravished eyes, – it calls thee up, present; and I see thee now!

Figure to yourself, Madam, a fair stripling, between eighteen and nineteen, with his head reclined on one of the sides of the chair, his hair in disordered curls, irregularly shading a face, on which all the roseate bloom of youth and all the manly graces conspired to fix my eyes and heart. Even the languor and paleness of his face, in which the momentary triumph of the lily over the rose was owing to the excesses of the night, gave an inexpressible sweetness to the finest features imaginable: his eyes closed in sleep, displayed the meeting

Rowlandson: Man Asleep on a Sofa (*detail*)

edges of their lids beautifully bordered with long eyelashes, over which no pencil could have described two more regular arches than those that graced his forehead, which was high, perfectly white and smooth; then a pair of vermillion lips, pouting and swelling to the touch, as if a bee had freshly stung them, seemed to challenge me to get the gloves of this lovely sleeper, had not the modesty and respect, which in both sexes are inseparable from a true passion, checked my impulses.

But on seeing his shirt collar unbuttoned, and a bosom whiter than a drift of snow, the pleasure of considering it could not bribe me to lengthen it at the hazard of a health that began to be my life's concern. Love, that made me timid, taught me to be tender too: with a trembling hand I took hold of one of his, and waking him as gently as possible, he started, and looking at first a little wildly, said, with a voice that sent its harmonious sound to my heart: 'Pray, child, what o'clock is it?' I told him and added that he might catch cold if he slept longer with his breast open in the cool of the morning air. On this he thanked me, with a sweetness perfectly agreeing with that of his features and eyes; the last now broad open, and eagerly surveying me, carried the sprightly fires they sparkled with directly to my heart.

It seems that having drunk too freely before he came upon the rake with some of his young companions, he had put himself out of a condition to go through all the weapons with them, and crown the night with getting a mistress; so that seeing me in a loose undress, he did not doubt but I was one of the misses of the house, sent in to repair his loss of time; but though he seized that notion, and a very obvious one it was, without hesitation, yet, whether my figure made a more than ordinary impression on him, or whether it was his natural politeness, he addressed me in a manner far from rude, though still on the foot of one of the house-pliers, come to amuse him; and giving me the first kiss that I ever relished from man in my life, asked me if I could favour him with my company, assuring me that he would make it worth my while. But had not even new-born love, that true refiner of lust, opposed so sudden a surrender, the fear of being surprised by the house was a sufficient bar to my compliance.

I told him then, in a tone set me by love itself, that for reasons I had not time to explain to him, I could not stay with him, and might not even ever see him again, with a sigh at these last words which broke from the bottom of my heart. My conqueror, who, as he afterwards told me, had been struck with my appearance, and liked me as much as he could think of liking anyone in my supposed way of life, asked me briskly at once if I would be kept by him, and that he would take a lodging for me directly, and relieve me from any engagements he presumed I might be under to the house. Rash, sudden, undigested, and even dangerous as this offer might be from a perfect stranger, and that stranger a giddy boy, the prodigious love I was struck with for him had put a charm into his voice there was no resisting, and blinded me to every objection: I could, at that instant, have died for him; think if I could resist an invitation to live with him! Thus my heart, beating strong to the proposal, dictated my answer, after scarce a minute's pause, that I would accept of his offer, and make my escape to him, in what way he pleased, and that I would be entirely at his disposal, let it be good or bad. I have often since wondered that so great an easiness did not disgust him, or make me too cheap in his eyes; but my fate had so appointed it that in his fears of the hazard of the town, he had been some time looking out for a girl to take into keeping, and my person happening to hit his fancy, it was by one of those miracles reserved to love that we struck the bargain in the instant, which we sealed by an exchange of kisses, that the hopes of a more uninterrupted enjoyment engaged him to content himself with.

Never, however, did dear youth carry in his person more wherewith to justify the turning of a girl's head, and making her set all consequences at defiance for the sake of following a gallant.

For besides all the perfections of manly beauty which were assembled in his form, he had an air of neatness and gentility, a certain smartness in the carriage and port of his head, that yet more distinguished him: his eyes were sprightly and full of meaning; his looks had in them something at once sweet and commanding. His complexion out-bloomed the lovely coloured rose, whilst its inimitable tender vivid glow clearly saved it from the reproach of wanting life, of raw and dough-like, which is commonly made to those so extremely fair as he was.

Our little plan was that I should get out about seven the next morning (which I could readily promise, as I knew where to get the key of the street-door), and he would wait at the end of the street with a coach to convey me safe off; after which he would send and clear any debt incurred by my stay at Mrs Brown's, who he only judged, in gross, might not care to part with one he thought so fit to draw custom to the house.

I then just hinted to him not to mention in the house his having seen such a person as me, for reasons I would explain to him more at leisure. And then, for fear of miscarrying by being seen together, I tore myself from him with a bleeding heart, and stole up softly to my room, where I found Phoebe still fast alseep, and hurrying off my few clothes, lay down by her, with a mixture of joy and anxiety that may be easier conceived than expressed.

The risks of Mrs Brown's discovering my purpose, of disappointments, misery, ruin, all vanished before this new-kindled flame. The seeing, touching, the being, if but for a night, with this idol of my fond virgin-heart appeared to me a happiness above the purchase of my liberty or life. He might use me ill! Let him! He was the master! Happy, too happy, even to receive death at so dear a hand.

To this purpose were the reflections of the whole day, of which every minute seemed to me a little eternity. How often did I visit the clock, nay, was tempted to advance the tedious hand, as if that would have advanced the time with it! Had those of the house made the least observations on me, they must have remarked something extraordinary from the discomposure I could not help betraying: especially when at dinner mention was made of the charmingest youth having been there, and stayed breakfast! Oh, he was such a beauty! I should have died for him! They would pull caps for him! and the

Philip Mercier: Portrait of a Gentleman

like fooleries, which, however, was throwing oil on a fire I was sorely put to it to smother the blaze of.

The fluctuations of my mind, the whole day, produced however one good effect; which was that through mere fatigue I slept tolerably well till five in the morning, when I got up, and having dressed myself, waited, under the double tortures of fear and impatience, for the appointed hour. It came at last, the dear, critical, dangerous hour came; and now supported only by the courage love lent me, I ventured a-tip-toe downstairs, leaving my box behind, for fear of being surprised with it in going out.

I got to the street-door, the key whereof was always laid on the chair by our bedside, in trust with Phoebe, who, having not the least suspicion of my entertaining any design to go from them (nor indeed had I but the day before), made no reserve or concealment of it from me. I opened the door then with great ease; love, that emboldened, protected me too: and now, got safe into the street, I saw my new guardian angel waiting at a coach-door ready open. How I got to him I know not; I suppose I flew; but I was in the coach in a trice, and he by the side of me, with his arms clasped around me, and giving me the kiss of welcome. -The coachman had his orders, and drove to them.

My eyes were instantly filled with tears, but tears of the most delicious delight. To find myself in the arms of that beauteous youth was a rapture that my little heart swam in. Past or future were equally out of the question with me. The present was as much as all powers of life were sufficient to bear the transport of without fainting. Nor were the most tender embraces,the most soothing expressions wanting on his side to assure me of his love, and of never giving me cause to repent the bold step I had taken in throwing myself thus entirely upon his honour and generosity. But, alas! This was no merit in me, for I was driven to it by a passion too impetuous for me to resist, and I did what I did because I could not help it.

In an instant, for time was now annihilated with me, we were landed at a public house in Chelsea, hospitably commodious for the reception of duet parties of pleasure, where a breakfast of chocolate was prepared for us.

An old jolly stager, who kept it, and understood life perfectly well, breakfasted with us, and leering archly at me, gave us both joy, and said we were well paired, i'faith! that a great many gentlemen and ladies used his house, but he had never seen a handsomer couple, . . . he was sure I was a fresh piece . . . I looked so country, so innocent! well, my spouse was a lucky man! . . . all which common landlord's cant not only pleased and soothed me, but helped to divert my confusion at being with my new sovereign, whom, now the minute approached, I began to fear to be alone with, a timidity which true love had a greater share in than even maiden bashfulness.

I wished, I doted, I could have died for him, and yet I know not how or why I dreaded the point which had been the object of my fiercest wishes; my pulses beat fears, amidst a flush of the warmest desires: this struggle of the passions, however, this conflict betwixt modesty and love-sick longings, made me burst again into tears, which he took, as he had done before, only for the remains of concern and emotion at the suddenness of my change of condition, in committing myself to his care, and in consequence of that idea, did and said all that he thought would most comfort and re-inspirit me.

After breakfast, Charles, the dear familiar name I must take the liberty henceforward to distinguish my Adonis by, with a smile full of meaning, took me gently by the hand and said, 'Come, my dear, and I will show you a room that commands a fine prospect over some gardens.' And without waiting for an answer, in which he relieved me extremely, he led me up into a chamber, airy and lightsome, where all seeing of prospects was out of the question, except that of a bed, which had all the air of having recommended the room to him.

Charles had just slipped the bolt of the door, and running, caught me in his arms, and lifting me from the ground with his lips glued to mine, bore me, trembling, panting, dying with soft fears and tender wishes, to the bed, where his impatience would not suffer him to undress me more than just unpinning my handkechief and gown, and unlacing my stays.

My bosom was now bare, and rising in the warmest throbs, presented to his sight and feeling the firm hard swell of a pair of young breasts, such as may be imagined of a girl not sixteen, fresh out of the country, and never before handled; but even their pride, whiteness, fashion, pleasing resistance to the touch, could not bribe his restless hands from roving. But giving them the loose, my petticoats and shift were soon taken up, and their stronger center of attraction laid open to their tender invasion. My fears, however, made me mechanically close my thighs; but the very touch of his hand insinuated between them disclosed them and opened a way for the main attack.

In the meantime I lay fairly exposed to the examination of his eyes and hands, quiet and unresisting, which confirmed him in the opinion he proceeded so cavalierly upon, that I was no novice in these matters, since he had taken me out of a common bawdy-house; nor had I said one thing to

William Hogarth: Before

William Hogarth: After

prepossess him of my virginity; and if I had, he would sooner have believed that I took him for a cully that would swallow such an improbability than that I was still mistress of that darling treasure, that hidden mine, so eagerly sought after by the men, and which they never dig for but to destroy.

Being now too high wound up to bear a delay, he unbuttoned, and drawing out the engine of love-assaults, drove it currently as at a ready-made breach. Then! then! for the first time did I feel that stiff horn-hard gristle battering against the tender part; but imagine to yourself his surprise when he found, after several vigorous pushes, which hurt me extremely, that he made not the least impression.

I complained, but tenderly complained I could not bear it . . . indeed! he hurt me. Still he thought no more than that being so young, the largeness of his machine (for few men could dispute size with him) made all the difficulty, and that possibly I had not been enjoyed by any so advantageously made in that part as himself; for still, that my virgin flower was yet uncropped never once entered into his head, and he would have thought it idling with time and words to have questioned me upon it.

He tries again; still no admittance; still no penetration; but he had hurt me yet more, whilst my extreme love made me bear extreme pain almost without a groan: at length, after repeated fruitless trials, he lay down panting by me, kissed my falling tears and asked me tenderly what was the meaning of so much complaining, and if I had not born it better from others than I did from him? I answered, with a simplicity framed to persuade, that he was the first man that ever served me so. Truth is powerful, and it is not always that we do not believe what we eagerly wish.

Charles, already disposed by the evidence of his senses to think my pretences to virginity not entirely apocryphal, smothers me with kisses, begs me, in the name of love, to have a little patience, and that he will be as tender of hurting me as he would be of himself.

Alas! it was enough I knew his pleasure, to submit joyfully to him, whatever pain I foresaw it would cost me.

He now resumes his attempts in more form: first he put one of the pillows under me, to give the blank of his aim a more favourable elevation, and another under my head, in ease of it; then, spreading my thighs, and placing himself standing between them, made them rest upon his hips; applying then the point of his machine to the slit, into which he sought entrance; it was so small he could scarce assure himself of its being rightly pointed. He looks, he feels, and satisfies himself; then driving forward with fury, its prodigious stiffness thus impacted, wedge-like, breaks the union of those parts and gained him just the insertion of the tip of it, lip-deep which, being sensible of, he improves his advantage, and following well his stroke, in a straight line, forcibly deepens his penetration, but put me to such intolerable pain, from the separation of the sides of that soft passage by a hard thick body, I could have screamed out; but unwilling as I was to alarm the house, I held in my breath and crammed my petticoat (which was turned up over my face) into my mouth, and bit it through in the agony. At length, the tender texture of that tract giving way to such fierce tearing and rending, he pierced something further into me: and now, outrageous, and no longer his own master, but borne headlong away by the fury and over-mettle of that member now exerting itself with a kind of native rage, he breaks in, carries all before him, and one violent merciless lunge sent it, imbrued and reeking with virgin blood, up to the very hilts in me: then! then! all my resolution deserted me; I screamed out and fainted away with the sharpness of the pain; and (as he told me afterwards), on his drawing out, when emission was over with him, my thighs were instantly all in a stream of blood that flowed from the wounded torn passage.

When I recovered my senses, I found myself undressed and abed, in the arms of the sweet relenting murderer of my virginity, who hung mourning tenderly over me, and holding in his hands a cordial, which, coming from the still dear author of so much pain I could not refuse. My eyes, however, moistened with tears and languishingly turned upon him, seemed to reproach him with his cruelty, and ask him if such were the rewards of love. But Charles, to whom I was now infinitely endeared, by his complete triumph over a maidenhead, where he so little expected to find one, in tenderness to that pain which he had put me to in procuring himself the height of pleasure, smothered his exultation and employed himself with so much sweetness, so much warmth, to sooth, to caress, and comfort me in my soft complainings, that breathed indeed more love than resentment, that I presently drowned all sense of pain in the pleasure of seeing him, of thinking that I belonged to him, he who now was the absolute disposer of my happiness, and, in one word, my fate.

The sore was however too tender, the wound too bleeding fresh, for Charle's good nature to put my patience presently to another trial; but as I could not stir or walk across the room, he ordered the dinner to be brought to the bedside, where it could not be otherwise than my getting down the wing of a fowl, and two or three glasses of wine, since it was my adored youth who both served and urged them on me, with that sweet irresistible authority with which love had invested him over me.

After dinner, and every thing but the wine taken away, Charles very impudently asks a leave he might read the grant of in my eyes, to come to bed to me, and accordingly falls to undressing; which I could not see the progress of without strange emotions of fear and pleasure.

He is now in bed with me the first time, and in broad day; but when thrusting up his own shirt and my shift, he laid his naked glowing body to mine – oh! insupportable delight! oh! superhumane rapture! What pain could stand before a pleasure so transporting? I felt no more the smart of my wounds below; but, curling round him like the tendril of a vine, as if I feared any part of him should be untouched or unpressed by me, I returned his strenuous embraces and kisses with a fervour and gust only known to true love, and which mere lust could never rise to.

Yes, even at this time that all the tyranny of the passions is fully over and that my veins roll no longer but a cold tranquil stream, the remembrance of those passages that most affected me in my youth still cheers and refreshes me. Let me proceed then – my beauteous youth was now glued to me in all the folds and twists that we could make our bodies meet in: when no longer able to rein in the fierceness of refreshed desires, he gives his steed the head, and, gently insinuating his thighs between mine, stopping my mouth with kisses of humid fire, makes a fresh irruption, and renewing his thrusts, pierces, tears, and forces his way up the torn tender folds of the sheath that yielded him admission with a smart little less severe than when the breach was first made. I stifled, however, my cries, and bore him with the passive fortitude of an heroine; soon his thrusts, more and more furious, cheeks flushed with a deeper scarlet, his eyes turned up in the fervent fit and rolling nothing but their whites, some dying sighs and an agonizing shudder, announced the appoaches of that ecstatic pleasure I was yet in too much pain to come in for my share of.

Nor was it till after a few enjoyments had numbed and blunted the sense of the smart, and giving me to feel the titillating inspersion of balsamic sweets, drew from me the delicious return, and brought down all my passion, that I arrived at excess of pleasure through excess of pain; but when successive engagements had broken and inured me, I began to enter into the true

Jean-Honoré Fragonard: The Kiss

unallayed relish of that pleasure of pleasures, when the warm gush darts through all the ravished inwards. What floods of bliss! what melting transports! what agonies of delight! too fierce, too mighty for nature to sustain: well has she therefore, no doubt, provided the relief of a delicious momentary dissolution, the approaches of which are intimated by a dear delirium, a sweet thrill, on the point of emitting those liquid sweets in which enjoyment itself is drowned, when one gives the languishing stretch-out and dies at the discharge.

How often, when the rage and tumult of my senses has subsided after the melting flow, have I, in a tender meditation, asked myself coolly the question, if it was in nature for any of its creatures to be so happy as I was? Or, what were all the fears of my future fate, put in the scale of one night's enjoyment of anything so transcendently the taste of my eyes and heart, as that delicious, fond, matchless youth?

Thus we spent the whole afternoon, till supper-time, in a continued circle of love-delights, kissing, turtle-billing, toying, and all the rest of the feast. At length, supper was served in, before which Charles had, for I do not know what reason, slipped his clothes on, and sitting down by the bedside, we made table and tablecloth of the bed and sheets, whilst he suffered nobody to attend or serve but himself. He ate with a very good appetite, and seemed charmed to see me eat. For my part, I was so enchanted with my fortune, so transported with the comparison of the delights I now swarmed in, with all the insipidity of my past scenes of life, that I thought them sufficiently cheap at even the price of my ruin, or the risque of their not lasting. The present possession was all my little head could find room for.

We lay together that night, when after playing repeated prizes of pleasure, nature, overspent and satisfied, gave us up to the arms of sleep; those of my dear youth encircled me, the consciousness of which made even that sleep more delicious.

Late in the morning I waked first; and observing my lover slept profoundly, softly disengaged myself from his arms, scarcely daring to breath, for fear of shortening his repose; my cap, my hair, my shift were all in disorder from the rufflings I had undergone; and I took this opportunity to adjust and set them as well as I could, whilst every now and then, looking at the sleeping youth with inconceivable fondness and delight, and reflecting on all the pain he had put me to, tacitly owned that the pleasure had overpaid me for my sufferings.

It was then broad day. I was sitting up in the bed, the clothes of which were all tossed, or rolled off, by the unquietness of our motions, from the sultry heat of the weather; nor could I refuse myself a pleasure that sollicited me so irresistibly, as this fair occasion of feasting my sight with all those treasures of youthful beauty I had enjoyed, and which lay now almost entirely naked, his shirt being trussed up in a perfect wisp, which the warmth of the room and season made me easy about the consequence of. I hung over him enamoured indeed! and devoured all his naked charms with only two eyes, when I could have wished them at least a hundred, for the fuller enjoyment of the gaze.

Oh! could I paint his figure as I see it now still present to my transported imagination! A whole length of an all-perfect manly beauty in full view. Think of a face without a fault, glowing with all the opening bloom and vernal freshness of an age in which beauty is of either sex, and which the first down over his upper-lip scarce began to distinguish.

The parting of the double ruby pout of his lips seemed to exhale an air sweeter and purer than what it drew in: ah! what violence did it not cost to refrain the so tempted kiss!

Then a neck exquisitely turned, graced behind and on the sides with his hair playing freely in natural ringlets, connected his head to a body of the most perfect form, and of the most vigorous contexture, in which all the strength of manhood was concealed and softened to appearance by the delicacy of his complexion, the smoothness of his skin, and the plumpness of his flesh.

The platform of his snow-white bosom, that was laid out in a manly proportion, presented, on the vermillion summet of each pap, the idea of a rose about to blow.

Nor did his shirt hinder from observing that symmetry of his limbs, that exactness of shape, in the fall of it towards the loins, where the waist ends and the rounding swell of the hips commences, where the skin, sleek, smooth, and dazzling white, burnishes on the stretch over firm, plump-ripe flesh, that crimped and run into dimples at the least pressure, or that the touch could not rest upon, but slid over as on the surface of the most polished ivory.

His thighs finely fashioned, and with a florid glossy roundness gradually tapering away to the knees, seemed pillars worthy to support that beauteous frame, at the bottom of which I could not, without some remains of terror, some tender emotions too, fix my eyes on that terrible spitfire machine, which had, not so long before, with such fury broke into, torn, and almost ruined those soft tender parts of mine, which had not yet done smarting with the effects of its rage; but behold it now! crest-fallen, reclining its half-capped vermillion head over one of his thighs, quiet, pliant, and to all appearance incapable of the mischiefs and cruelty it had committed. Then the beautiful growth of the hair, in short and soft curls round its root, its whiteness, branched veins, the supple softness of the shaft, as it lay foreshortened, rolled and shrunk up into a squob thickness, languid, and born up from between the thighs by its globular appendage, that wondrous treasure-bag of nature's sweets, which, rivelled round and pursed up in the only wrinkles that are known to please, perfected the prospect, and all together formed the most interesting moving picture in nature, and surely infinitely superior to those nudities furnished by the painters, statuaries, or any art, which are purchased at immense prices, whilst the sight of them in actual life is scarce sovereignly tasted by any but the few whom nature has endowed with a fire of imagination, warmly pointed by a truth of judgement to the spring-head, the originals of beauty of nature's unequalled composition, above all the imitations of art, or the reach of wealth to pay their price.

But everything must have an end. A motion made by this angelic youth, in the listlessness of going-off sleep, replaced his shirt and clothes in a posture that shut up that treasury from longer view.

I lay down then, and carrying my hands to that part of me in which the objects just seen had begun to raise a mutiny that prevailed over the smart of them, my fingers now opened themselves an easy passage; but long I had not the time to consider the wide differences *there*, between the maid and the now finished woman, before Charles waked, and turning towards me, kindly inquired how I had rested, and scarce giving me time to answer, imprinted on my lips one of his burning rapture-kisses, which darted a flame to my heart, that from thence radiated to every part of me: and presently, as if he had proudly meant revenge for the survey I had smuggled of all his naked beauties, he spurns off the bedclothes, and trussing up my shift as high as it would go, took his turn to feast his eyes with all the gifts nature had bestowed on my person; his busy hands too ranged intemperantly over every part of me. The delicious austerity and hardness of my yet unripe budding breasts, the whiteness and firmness of my flesh, the freshness and regularity of my features, the harmony of my limbs, all seemed to confirm him in his satisfaction with his bargain: but, when curious to explore the havoc he had made in the tender center of his over-fierce attack, he not only directed his hands there, but with a pillow put under, placed me favourably for his wanton purpose of inspection; then, who can express the fire his eyes glistened, his hands glowed with, whilst sighs of pleasure, and tender broken exclamations were all the praises he could utter. By this time his machine, stiffly risen at me, lifted and bore the flap of his shirt out, which, presently fiercely removing, gave me to see it in its highest state and bravery: He feels it himself, seems pleased at its condition, and, smiling loves and graces, seizes one of my hands, and carries it, with a gentle compulsion, to this pride of nature, and its richest masterpiece.

I, struggling faintly, could not help feeling what I could not grasp, a column of the whitest ivory, beautifully streaked with blue veins, and carrying, fully uncapped, a head of the liveliest vermillion: no horn could be harder or stiffer; yet no velvet more smooth or delicious to the touch. Presently he guided my hand lower, to that part in which nature and pleasure keep their stores in concert, so aptly fastened and hung on to the root of their first instrument and minister, that not improperly he might be styled their purse-bearer too: there he made me feel distinctly, through their soft cover, the contents, a pair of roundish balls, that seemed to play within, and elude all pressure but the tenderest, from without.

But now this visit of my soft warm hand in those so sensible parts had put everything into such ungovernable fury that, disdaining all further preluding, and taking the advantage of my commodious posture, he made the storm fall where I scarce patiently expected, and where he was sure to lay it: presently then, I felt the stiff intersertion between the yielding divided lips of the wound now open for life; where the narrowness no longer put me to intolerable pain, and afforded my lover no more difficulty than what heightened his pleasure, in the strict embrace of that tender warm sheath, round the instrument it was so deliciously adjusted to, and which, now cased home, so gorged me with pleasure that it perfectly suffocated me and took away my breath; then the killing thrusts! the unnumbered kisses! every one of which was a joy inexpressible; and that joy lost in a crowd of yet greater blisses. But this was a disorder too violent in nature to last long: the vessels so stirred and intensely heated soon boiled over, and for that time put out the fire. Meanwhile all this dalliance and disport had so far consumed the morning that it became a kind of necessity to lay breakfast and dinner into one.

In our calmer intervals Charles gave the following account of himself, every title of which was true. He was the only son of a father who, having a small post in the revenue, rather overlived his income and had given this young gentleman a very slender education; no profession had he bred him up to, but designed to provide for him in the army by purchasing him an ensign's commission, that is to say, provided he could raise the money, or procure it by interest, either of which clauses was rather to be wished than hoped for by him. On no better a plan, however, than this had this improvident father suffered this youth, and a youth of great promise, to run up to the age of manhood, or near it at least, in next to idleness, and had besides taken no sort of pains to give him even the common premonitions against the vices of the town, and the dangers of all sorts which wait the unexperienced and unwary in it. He lived at home, and at discretion, with his father, who himself kept a mistress, and for the rest, provided Charles did not ask him for money, he was indolently kind to him: he might lie out when he pleased, any excuse would serve, and even his reprimands were so slight that they carried with them rather an air of connivance at the fault than any serious control or constraint. But, to supply his calls for money, Charles, whose mother was dead, had, by her side, a grandmother who doted upon and did not a little help spoil him. She had a considerable annuity to live upon, and very regularly parted with every shilling she could spare to this darling of her's, to the no little heartburn of his father, who was vexed, not that she by this means fed his son's extravagance, but that she preferred Charles to himself; and we shall too soon see what a fatal turn such a mercenary jealousy could operate on the breast of a father.

Charles was, however, by the means of his grandmother's lavish fondness, very sufficiently enabled to keep a mistress so easily contented as my love made me; and my good fortune, for such I must ever call it, threw me in his way, in the manner above related, just as he was on the look-out for one.

As to his temper, the even sweetness of it made him seem born for domestic happiness: tender, naturally polite, and gentle-mannered, it could never be his fault if ever jars or animosities ruffled a calm he was so qualified every way to maintain or restore. Without those great or shining qualities that constitute a genius, or are fit to make a noise in the world, he had all those humble ones that compose the softer social merit: plain common sense, set off with every grace of modesty and good nature, made him, if not admired, what is much happier, universally beloved and esteemed. But, as nothing but the beauties of his person had at first attracted my regard and fixed my passion, neither was I then a judge of that internal merit, which I had afterwards full occasion to discover, and which perhaps, in that season of giddiness and levity, would have touched my heart very little, had it been lodged in a person less the delight of my eyes and idol of my senses. But to return to our situation.

After dinner, which we ate abed in a most voluptuous disorder, Charles got up, and taking a passionate leave of me for a few hours, he went to town, where, concerting matters with a young sharp lawyer, they went together to my late venerable mistress's, from whence I had but the day before made my elopement, and with whom he was determined to settle accounts in a manner that should cut off all after-reckonings from that quarter.

Accordingly, they went; but by the way, the Templar, his friend, on thinking over Charles's information, saw reason to give their visit another turn, and instead of offering satisfaction, to demand it.

On being let in, the girls of the house flocked round Charles, whom they knew, and from the earliness of my escape, and their perfect ignorance of his ever having so much as seen me, not having the least suspicion of his being accessory to my flight, they were, in their way, *making up* to him; and as to his companion, they took him probably for a fresh cully. But the Templar soon checked their forwardness by inquiring for the old lady, with whom, he said, with a grave judge-like countenance, that he had some business to settle.

Madam was immediately sent for down, and the ladies being desired to clear the room, the lawyer asked her severely if she did not know or had not decoyed, under pretence of hiring as a servant, a young girl just come out of the country, called Frances or Fanny Hill, describing me withall as particularly as he could from Charles's description.

It is peculiar to vice to tremble at the inquiries of justice; and Mrs Brown, whose conscience was not entirely clear upon my account, as knowing as she was of the town, as hackneyed as she was in buffing through all the dangers of her vocation, could not help being alarmed at the question, especially when he went on to talk of a justice of peace, Newgate, the Old Bailey, indictments for keeping a disorderly house, pillory, carting, and the whole process of that nature: She, who, it is likely, imagined I had lodged an information against her house, looked extremely blank, and began to make a thousand protestations and excuses. However, to abridge, they brought away triumphantly my

P. Sandby: A Young Man

Rev. Matthew William Peters: Lydia

box of things, which, had she not been under an awe, she might have disputed with them; and not only that, but a clearance and discharge of any demands on the house, at the expense of no more than a bowl of arrack-punch, the treat of which, together with the choice of the house-conveniences, was offered, and not accepted. Charles all the time acted the chance companion of the lawyer, who had brought him there, as he knew the house, and appeared in no wise interested in the issue, but he had the collateral pleasure of hearing all I had told him verified, so far as the bawd's fears would give her leave to enter into my history, which, if one may guess by the composition she so readily came into, were not small.

Phoebe, my kind tutoress Phoebe, was at that time gone out, perhaps in search of me, or their cooked-up story had not, it is probable, passed so smoothly.

This negotiation had, however taken up some time, which would have appeared much longer to me, left as I was in a strange house, if the landlady, a motherly sort of woman to whom Charles had liberally recommended me, had not come up and borne me company. We drank tea, and her chat helped to pass away the time very agreeably, since he was our theme; but as the evening deepened, and the hour set for his return was elapsed, I could not dispel the gloom of impatience and tender fears which gathered upon me, and which our timid sex are apt to feel in proportion to their love.

Long, however, I did not suffer, the sight of him overpaid me; and the soft reproach I had prepared for him expired before it reached my lips.

I was still abed, yet unable to use my legs otherwise than awkwardly, and Charles flew to me, catches me in his arms, raised, and, extending mine to meet his dear embrace, gives me an account, interrupted by many a sweet parenthesis of kisses, of the success of his measures.

I could not help laughing at the fright the old woman had been put into, which my ignorance, and indeed my want of innocence, had far from prepared me for bespeaking. She had, it seems, apprehended that I had fled for shelter to some relation I had recollected in town, on my dislike of their ways and proceeding towards me, and that this application came from thence. For, as Charles had rightly judged, not one neighbour had, at that still hour, seen the circumstance of my escape into the coach, or at least noticed him; neither had any in the house the least hint or clue of suspicion of my having spoke to him, much less of my having clapped up such a sudden bargain with a perfect stranger: thus the greatest improbability is not always what we should most mistrust.

We supped with all the gaiety of two young giddy creatures at the top of their desires; and as I had most joyfully given up to Charles the whole charge of my future happiness, I thought of nothing beyond the exquisite pleasure of possessing him.

He came to bed in due time, and this second night, the pain being pretty well over, I tasted, in full draughts, all the transports of perfect enjoyment. I swam, I bathed in bliss, till both fell fast asleep, through the natural consequences of satisfied desires and appeased flames; nor did we wake but to renewed raptures.

Thus, making the most of love and life, did we stay at this lodging in Chelsea about ten days, in which time Charles took care to give his excursions from home a colourable gloss, and to keep his footing with his fond, indulgent grandmother, from whom he drew constant and sufficient supplies for the charge I was to him, and which was very trifling, in comparison with his former less regular course of pleasures.

Charles removed me then to a private ready-furnished lodging in D – street, St James's, where he paid half a guinea a week for two rooms and a closet on the second floor, which he had been some time looking out for, and was more convenient for the frequency of his visits than where he had at first placed me, in a house which I cannot say but I left with regret, as it was infinitely endeared to me by the first possession of my Charles, and the circumstance of losing there that jewel which can never be twice lost. The landlord, however, had no reason to complain of anything but of a procedure in Charles too liberal not to make him regret his loss of us.

Arrived at our new lodgings, I remember I thought them extremely fine, though ordinary enough even at that price; but had it been a dungeon that Charles had brought me to, his presence would have made it a little Versailles.

The landlady, Mrs Jones. waited on us to our apartment, and, with great volubility of tongue, explained to us all its conveniences: that her own maid should wait on us – that the best quality had lodged at her house – that her first floor was let to a foreign secretary of an embassy and his lady – that I looked like a very good-natured lady. At the word lady, I blushed out of flattered vanity: this was too strong for a girl of my condition; for though Charles had had the precaution of dressing me in a less tawdry flaunting style than were the clothes I escaped to him in, and of passing me for his wife that he had secretly married and kept private (the old story) on account of his friends, I dare swear this appeared extremely apocryphal to a woman who knew the town as well as she did; but that was the least of her concern. It was impossible to be less scruple-ridden than she was; and the advantage of letting her rooms being her sole object, the truth itself would have far from scandalized her, or broken her bargain.

A sketch of her picture and personal history will dispose you to account for the part she is to act in my concerns.

She was about forty-six years old, tall, meagre, red-haired, with one of those trivial ordinary faces you meet with everywhere, and go about unheeded and unmentioned. In her youth she had been kept by a gentleman, who, dying, left her forty pounds a year during her life, in consideration of a daughter he had by her; which daughter, at the age of seventeen, she sold, for not a very considerable sum neither, to a gentleman who was going on envoy abroad and took his purchase with him, where he used her with the utmost tenderness, and, it is thought, was secretly married to her; but had constantly made a point of her not keeping up the least correspondence with a mother base enough to make a market of her own flesh and blood. However, as she had no nature, nor indeed any passion but that of money, this gave her no further uneasiness than as she thereby lost a handle of squeezing presents, or other after-advantages, out of the bargain. Indifferent then, by nature or constitution, to every other pleasure but that of increasing the lump by any means whatever, she commenced a kind of private procuress, for which she was not amiss fitted by her grave decent appearance, and sometimes did a job in the matchmaking way; in short, there was nothing that appeared to her under the shape of gain that she would not have undertaken. She knew most of the ways of the town, having not only herself been upon but kept up constant intelligences in it, dealing, besides her practice in promoting a harmony between the two sexes, in private prawn-broking and their profitable secrets. She rented the house she lived in and made the most of it by letting it out in lodgings; and though she was worth, at least, near three or four thousand pounds, she would not allow herself even the necessaries of life, and pinned her subsistence entirely on what she could squeeze out of her lodgers.

When she saw such a young pair come under her roof, her immediate notions doubtless were how she should make the most money of us, by every means that money might be made, and which she rightly judged our situation and inexperience would soon beget her occasions of.

In this hopeful sanctuary, and under the clutches of this harpy, did we pitch our residence. It will not be mighty material to you, or very pleasant to me, to enter into a detail of all the petty cut-throat ways and means with which she used to fleece us; all which Charles indolently chose to bear with, rather than take the trouble of removing, the difference of the expense being scarce attended to by a young gentleman who had no ideas of stint, or even economy, and a raw country girl who knew nothing of the matter.

Here, however, under the wings of my sovereignly beloved, did I flow the most delicious hours of my life; my Charles I had, and in him every thing my fond heart could wish or desire. He carried me to plays, operas, masquerades and every diversion of the town, all which pleased me indeed, but pleased me infinitely the more for his being with me, and explaining everything to me, and enjoying perhaps the natural impressions of surprise and admiration, which such sights at the first never fail to excite in a country girl new to the delights of them. But to me, they sensibly proved the power and full dominion of the sole passion of my heart over me, a passion in which soul and body were concentered and left me no room for any other relish of life but love.

As to the men I saw at those places, or at any other, they suffered so much in the comparison my eyes made of them with my all-perfect Adonis that I had not the infidelity even of one wandering thought to reproach myself with upon his account. He was the universe to me, and all that was not him was nothing to me.

My love, in fine, was so excessive that it arrived at annihilating every suggestion or kindling spark of jealousy, for, one idea only tending that way gave me such exquisite torment that my self-love and dread of worse than death made me for ever renounce and defy it: nor had I indeed occasion, for, were I to enter here on a recital of several instances wherein Charles sacrificed to me women of greater importance than I dare hint (which, considering his form, was no such wonder), I might indeed give you full proof of his unshaken constancy to me, but would not you accuse me of warming up again a feast that my vanity ought long ago to have been satisfied with?

In our cessations from active pleasure, Charles framed himself one, in instructing me, as far as his own lights reached, in a great many points of life that I was, in consequence of my no-education, perfectly ignorant of. Nor did I suffer one word to fall in vain from the mouth of my lovely teacher; I hung on every syllable he uttered, and received as oracles all he said, whilst kisses

Thomas Rowlandson: The Larking Cull

were all the interruption I could not refuse myself the pleasure of admitting, from lips that breathed more than Arabian sweetness.

I was in a little time enabled, by the progress I had made, to prove the deep regard I had paid to all that he had said to me; repeating it to him almost word for word, and to show that I was not entirely the parrot, but that I reflected upon, that I entered into it, I joined my own comments and asked him questions of explanation.

My country accent and the rusticity of my gait, manner, and deportment began now sensibly to wear off, so quick was my observation, and so efficacious my desire of growing every day worthier of his heart.

As to money, though he brought me constantly all he received, it was with difficulty he even got me to give it room in my bureau, and what clothes I had, he could prevail on me to accept of on no other foot than that of pleasing him by the greater neatness in my dress, beyond which I had no ambition; I could have made a pleasure of the greatest toil, and worked my fingers to the bone, with joy, to have supported him: guess then, if I could harbour any idea of being burdensome to him: and this disinterested turn in me was so unaffected, so much the dictate of my heart, that Charles could not but feel it, and if he did not love me as much as I did him (which was the constant and only matter of sweet contention between us), he managed so at least as to give me the satisfaction of believing it impossible for man to be more tender, more true, more faithful than he was.

Our landlady, Mrs Jones, came frequently up to my apartment, from whence I never stirred on any pretext without Charles; nor was it long before she wormed out, without much art, the secret of our having cheated the church of a ceremony, and, in course, the terms we lived together upon: a circumstance which far from displeased her, considering the designs she had upon me, and which, alas! she will have too soon room to carry into execution. But in the meantime, her own experience of life let her see that any attempt, however indirect or disguised, to divert or break, at least presently, so strong a cement of hearts as ours was, could only end in losing two lodgers of whom she made very competent advantages, if either of us came to smoke her commission, for a commission she had from one of her customers, either to debauch or get me away from my keeper at any rate.

But the barbarity of my fate soon saved her the task of disuniting us. I had now been eleven months with this life of my life, which had passed in one continued rapid stream of delight; but nothing so violent was ever made to

Hogarth: The Harlot's Progress, plate 2

last. I was about three months gone with child by him, a circumstance which would have added to his tenderness, had he ever left me room to believe it could receive an addition, when the mortal, the unexpected blow of separation fell upon us. I shall gallop post over the particulars, which I shudder yet to think of, and cannot to this instant reconcile myself to how, or by what means, I could outlive it.

Two live-long days had I lingered through, without hearing from him, I, who breathed, who existed but in him, and had never yet seen twenty-four hours pass without seeing or hearing from him. The third day my impatience was so strong, my alarms had been so severe, that I perfectly sickened with them; and being unable to support the shock longer, I sunk upon the bed, and ringing for Mrs Jones, who had far from comforted me under my anxieties, she came up, and I had scarce breath and spirit enough to find words to beg of her if she would save my life, to fall upon some means of finding out instantly what was become of its only prop and comfort. She pitied me in a way that

Samuel Scott: Covent Garden Piazza and Market (*detail*)

rather sharpened my affliction than suspended it, and went out upon this commission.

For she had but to go to Charles's house, who lived but an easy distance, in one of the streets that run into Covent-Garden. There she went into a public-house, and from thence sent for a maid-sevant whose name I had given her, as the properest to inform her.

The maid readily came, and as readily, when Mrs Jones inquired of her what was become of Mr Charles, or whether he was gone out of town, acquainted her with the disposal of her master's son, which the very day after was no secret to the servants; such sure measures had he taken for the most cruel punishment of his child for having more interest with his grandmother than he had, though he made use of a pretence, plausible enough to get rid of him in this secret and abrupt manner, for fear her fondness should have interposed a bar to his leaving England, and proceeding on a voyage he had concerted for him, which pretext was that it was indispensably necessary to secure a considerable inheritance that devolved to him by the death of a rich merchant (his own brother) at one of the factories in the South Seas, of which he had lately received advice, together with a copy of the will.

In consequence of which resolution to send away his son, he had, unknown to him, made the necessary preparations for fitting him out, struck a bargain with the captain of a ship, whose punctual execution of his orders he had secured by his interest with his principal owner and patron, and, in short, concerted his measures so secretly and effectually that whilst his son thought he was going down the river, that would take him a few hours, he was stopped on board of a ship, debarred from writing, and more strictly watched than a state criminal.

Thus was the idol of my soul torn from me, and forced on a long voyage, without taking leave of one friend, or receiving one line of comfort, except a dry explanation and instructions from his father how to proceed when he should arrive at his destined port, enclosing withal some letters of recommendation to a factor there: all these particulars I did not learn minutely till some time after.

The maid, at the same time, added that she was sure this usage of her sweet young master would be the death of his grandmama, as indeed it proved true, for the old lady, on hearing it, did not survive the news a whole month; and as her fortune consisted in an annuity, out of which she had laid up no reserves, she left nothing worth mentioning to her so fatally envied darling, but absolutely refused to see his father before she died.

When Mrs Jones returned, and I observed her looks, they seemed so unconcerned and even nearest to pleased that I half flattered myself she was going to set my tortured heart at ease by bringing me good news; but this, indeed, was a cruel delusion of hope: the barbarian, with all the coolness imaginable, stabs me to the heart in telling me succinctly that he was sent away at least on a four years' voyage, (here she stretched maliciously) and that I could not expect in reason ever to see him again; and all this with such pregnant circumstances that I could not escape giving them credit, as in general they were indeed too true!

She had hardly finished her report before I fainted away, and after several successive fits, all the while wild and senseless, I miscarried of the dear pledge of my Charles's love: but the wretched never die when it is fittest that they should die, and women are hard-lived to a proverb.

The cruel and interested care taken to recover me saved an odious life: which, instead of the happiness and joys it had overflowed in, all of a sudden presented no view before me of anything but the depth of misery, horror, and the sharpest affliction.

Thus I lay six weeks, in the struggles of youth and constitution against the friendly efforts of death, which I constantly invoked to my relief and deliverance, but which, proving too weak for my wish, I recovered at length, but into a state of stupefaction and despair that threatened me with a loss of my senses, and a mad-house.

Time, however, that great comforter in ordinary, began to assuage the violence of my suffering, and to numb my feeling of them. My health returned to me, though I still retained an air of grief, dejection, and languor, which, taking off from the ruddiness of my country complexion, rendered it rather more delicate and affecting.

The landlady had all this time officiously provided and seen that I wanted for nothing, and as soon as she saw me retrieved into a condition of answering her purpose, one day after we had dined together, she congratulated me on my recovery, the merit of which she took entirely to herself, and all this by way of introduction to a most terrible and scurvy epilogue: 'You are now,' says she, 'Miss Fanny, tolerably well, and you are very welcome to stay in these lodgings as long as you please, you see I have asked you for nothing this long time, but truly I have a call to make up a sum of money which must be answered,' and, with that, presents me with a bill for arrears of rent, diet.

apothecary's charges, nurse, &c. sum total twenty-three pounds, seventeen and six-pence, towards discharging of which I had not in the world (which she well knew) more than seven guineas, left by chance, of my dear Charles's common stock with me. At the same time she desired me to tell her what course I would take for payment. I burst out into a flood of tears, and told her my condition, that I would sell what few clothes I had, and that, for the rest, would pay her as soon as possible; but my distress being favourable to her views, only stiffened her the more. She told me very coolly that she was indeed sorry for my misfortunes, but that she must do herself justice, though it would go to the very heart of her to send such a tender young creature to prison; at the word 'prison' every drop of my blood chilled, and my fright acted so strongly upon me that, turning as pale and faint as a criminal at the first sight of his place of execution, I was on the point of swooning. My landlady who wanted only to terrify me to a certain point, and not to throw me into a state of body inconsistent with her designs upon it, began to soothe me again, and told me, in a tone composed to more pity and gentleness, that it would be my own fault if she was forced to proceed to such extremities, but she believed there was a friend to be found in the world who would make up matters to both our satisfactions, and that she would bring him to drink tea with us that very afternoon, when she hoped we would come to a right understanding in our affairs. To all this, not a word of answer; I sat mute, confounded, terrified.

Mrs Jones, however, judging rightly that it was her time to strike whilst the impressions were so strong upon me, left me to myself and to all the terrors of an imagination wounded to death by the idea of going to a prison, and, from a principle of self-preservation, snatching at every glimpse of redemption from it.

In this situation I sat near half an hour, swallowed up in grief and despair, when my landlady came in, and, observing a death-like dejection in my countenance, still in pursuance of her plan, put on a false pity, and bidding me be of good heart, things, she said, would not be so bad as I imagined, if I would be but my own friend, and closed with telling me she had brought a very honourable gentleman to drink tea with me, who would give me the best advice how to get rid of all my troubles; upon which, without waiting for a reply, she goes out and returns with this very honourable gentleman, whose very honourable procuress she had been on this as well as other occasions.

The gentleman, on his entering the room, made me a very civil bow, which

I had scarce strength, or presence of mind enough to return a curtsey to; when the landlady, taking upon her to do all the honours of this first interview (for I had never, that I remembered, seen the gentleman before), sets a chair for him, and another for herself. All this while not a word on either side: a stupid stare was all the face I could put on this strange visit.

The tea was made, and the landlady, unwilling, I suppose, to lose any time, observing my silence and shyness before this entire stranger: 'Come, Miss Fanny,' says she in a coarse familiar style and tone of authority, 'hold up your head, child, and do not let sorrow spoil that pretty face of yours. What! sorrows are only for a time. Come, be free, here is a worthy gentleman who has heard of your misfortunes and is willing to serve you – you must be better acquainted with him, do not you now stand upon your punctilios, and this and that, but make your market while you may.'

At this so delicate and eloquent harangue, the gentleman, who saw I looked frighted and amazed, and indeed incapable of answering, took her up for breaking things in so abrupt a manner, as rather to shock than incline to an acceptance of the good he intended me; then, addressing himself to me, told me he was perfectly acquainted with my whole story, and every cicumstance of my distress, which he owned was a cruel plunge for one of youth and beauty to fall into; that he had long taken a liking to my person, for which he appealed to Mrs Jones, there present, but finding me so deeply engaged to another, he had lost all hopes of succeeding, till he heard the sudden reverse of fortune that had happened to me, on which he had given particular orders to my landlady to see that I should want for nothing, and that, had he not been forced abroad to The Hague on affairs he could not refuse himself to, he would himself have attended me during my sickness; that on his return, which was but the day before, he had, on learning my recovery, desired my landlady's good offices to introduce him to me, and was as angry, at least, as I was shocked, at the manner in which she had conducted herself towards obtaining him that happiness. but that to show me how much he disowned her procedure, and how far he was from taking an ungenerous advantage of my situation, and from exacting any security for my gratitude, he would, before my face, that instant, discharge my debt entirely to my landlady and give me her receipt in full, after which I should be at liberty either to reject or grant his suit, as he was much above putting any force upon my inclinations.

Whilst he was exposing his sentiments to me, I ventured just to look up to him and observe his figure, which was that of a very well looking gentleman, well made, of about forty, dressed in a suit of plain clothes, with a large diamond ring on one of his fingers, the lustre of which played in my eyes, as he waved his hand in talking and raised my notions of his importance; in short, he might pass for what is commonly called a comely black man, with an air of distinction natural to his birth and condition.

To all his speeches, however, I answered only in tears that flowed plentifully to my relief, and, choking up my voice, excused me from speaking, very luckily, for I should not have known what to say.

The sight, however, moved him, as he afterwards told me, irresistibly, and by way of giving me some reason to be less powerfully afflicted, he drew out his purse, and calling for pen and ink, which the landlady was prepared for, paid her every farthing of her demand, independant of a liberal gratification, which was to follow unknown to me, and taking a receipt in full, very tenderly forced me to secure it, by guiding my hand, which he had thrust it into, as to make me passively put it into my pocket.

Still I continued in a state of stupidity, or melancholic despair, as my spirits could not yet recover from the violent shocks they had received, and the commode landlady had actually left the room, and me along with this strange gentleman, before I observed it, and then observed it without alarm, for I was now lifeless, and indifferent to everything.

The gentleman, however, no novice in affairs of this sort, drew near me, and under the pretence of comforting me, first with his handkerchief dried my tears as they ran down my cheeks; presently, he ventured to kiss me: on my part neither resistance nor compliance. I sat stock-still; and now looking on myself as bought by the payment that had been transacted before me, I did not care what became of my wretched body; and wanting life, spirits, or courage to oppose the least struggle, even that of the modesty of my sex, I suffered tamely whatever the gentleman pleased, who, proceeding insensibly from freedom to freedom, insinuated his hand between my handkerchief and bosom, which he handled at discretion. Finding thus no repulse, and that everything favoured beyond expectation the completion of his desires, he took me in his arms and bore me without life or motion to the bed, on which laying me gently down, and having me at what advantage he pleased, I did not so much as know what he was about, till recovering from a trance of lifeless insensibility, I found him buried in me, whilst I lay passive and innocent of the least sensation of pleasure: a death cold corpse could scarce have had less life or sense in it. As soon as he had thus pacified a passion, which had too little respected the condition I was in, he got off, and after recomposing the disorder of my clothes, employed himself with the utmost tenderness to calm the transports of remorse and madness at myself, with which I was seized, too late, I confess, for having suffered on that bed the embraces of an utter stranger. I tore my hair, wrung my hands, and beat my breast like a madwoman; but when my new master, for in that light I then viewed him, applied himself to appease me, as my whole rage was levelled at myself, no part of which I thought myself permitted to aim at him. I begged him, with more submission than anger, to leave me alone, that I might at least enjoy my affliction in quiet; this he positively refused, for fear, as he pretended, that I should do myself a mischief.

Violent passions seldom last long, and those of women least of any. A dead still calm succeeded this storm, which ended in a profuse shower of tears.

Had anyone, but a few instants before, told me that I should have ever known any man but Charles, I would have spat in his face, or had I been offered infinitely a greater sum of money than that I saw paid for me, I had spurned the proposal in cold blood. But our virtues and our vices depend too much on our circumstances: unexpectedly beset as I was, betrayed by a mind weakened by a long severe affliction, and stunned with the terrors of a gaol, my defeat will appear the more excusable, since I certainly was not present at, or a party in any sense, to it. However, as the first enjoyment is decisive, and he was now over the bar, I thought I had no longer a right to refuse the caresses of one that had got that advantage over me, no matter how obtained. Conforming myself then to this maxim, I considered myself as so much in his power that I endured his kisses and embraces without affecting struggles or anger; not that they as yet gave me any pleasure, or prevailed over the aversion of my soul to give myself up to any sensation of that sort; what I suffered, I suffered out of a kind of gratitude, and as matter of course after what had passed.

He was, however, so regardful as not to attempt the renewal of those extremities which had thrown me just before into such violent agitations; but, now secure of possession, contented himself with bringing me to temper by degrees, and waiting at the hand of time for those fruits of his generosity and courtship which he since often reproached himself with having gathered much too green, when, yielding to the invitations of my inability to resist him, and overborn by desires, he had wreaked his passion on a mere lifeless spiritless body, dead to all purposes of joy, since, taking none, it ought to have

Boucher: Bust of a Girl

been supposed incapable of giving any. This is, however, certain: my heart never thoroughly forgave him the manner in which I had fallen to him, although, in point of interest, I had reason to be pleased that he found in my person wherewithal to keep him from leaving me as easily as he had had me.

The evening was in the meantime so far advanced that the maid came in to lay the cloth for supper, when I understood with joy that my landlady, whose sight was present poison to me, was not to be with us.

Presently a neat and elegant supper was introduced, and a bottle of Burgundy, with the other necessaries, were set on a dumb-waiter.

The maid quitting the room, the gentleman insisted, with a tender warmth, that I should sit up in the elbow chair by the fire and see him eat, if I could not be prevailed on to eat myself. I obeyed, with a heart full of affliction, at the comparison it made between those delicious tête-à-têtes with my ever dear youth and this forced situation, this new awkward scene, imposed and obtruded on me by cruel necessity.

At supper, after a great many arguments used to comfort and reconcile me to my fate, he told me that his name was H – , brother to the earl of L – , and that, having by the suggestions of my landlady been led to see me, he had found me perfectly to his taste, had given her a commission to procure me at any rate, and that he had at length succeeded as much to his satisfaction as he passionately wished it might be to mine, adding withal some flattering assurances that I should have no cause to repent my knowledge of him.

I had now got down at least half a partidge, and three or four glasses of wine, which he compelled me to drink by way of restoring nature; but whether there was anything extraordinary put into the wine, or whether there wanted no more to revive the natural warmth of my constitution and give fire to the old train, I began no longer to look with that constraint, not to say disgust, on Mr H – , which I had hitherto done; but withal there was not the least grain of love mixed with this softening of my sentiments: any other man would have been just the same to me as Mr H – , that stood in the same circumstances and had done for me, and with me, what he had done.

There are not, on earth at least, eternal griefs; mine were, if not at an end, at least suspended: my heart, which had been so long overloaded with anguish and vexation, began to dilate and open to the least gleam of diversion, or amusement. I wept a little, and my tears relieved me; I sighed, and my sighs seemed to lighten me of a load that oppressed me; my countenance grew, if not cheerful, at least more composed and free.

Mr H –, who had watched, perhaps brought on, this change, knew too well not to seize it. He thrust the table imperceptibly from between us, and bringing his chair to face me, he soon began, after preparing me by all the endearments of assurances and protestations, to lay hold of my hands, to kiss me, and once more to make free with my bosom, which, being at full liberty from the disorder of my loose dishabille, now panted and throbbed, less with indignation than with fear and bashfulness at being used so familiarly by still a stranger; but he soon gave me greater occasion to exclaim, by stooping down and slipping his hand above my garters; thence he strove to regain the pass which he had before found so open and unguarded. But now he could not unlock the twist of my thighs: I gently complained and begged him to let me alone; told him I was not well; however, as he saw there was more form and ceremony in my resistance than good earnest, he made his conditions for desisting from pursuing his point that I should be put instantly to bed, whilst he gave certain orders to the landlady, and that he would return in an hour, when he hoped to find me more reconciled to his passion for me than I seemed at present. I neither assented nor denied, but in my air and manner of receiving this proposal gave him to see that I did not think myself enough my own mistress to refuse it.

Accordingly he went out and left me, when a minute or two after, before I could recover myself into any composure for thinking, the maid came in with her mistress's service, and a small silver porringer of what she called a bridal posset, and desired me to eat it as I went to bed, which consequently I did, and felt immediately a heat, a fire, run like a hue-and-cry through every part of my body; I burnt, I glowed, and wanted even little of wishing for any man.

The maid, as soon as I was lain down, took the candle away, and wishing me a good night, went out of the room and shut the door after her.

She had hardly time to get downstairs before Mr H – opened my room door softly, and came in, now undressed, in his nightgown and cap, with two lighted wax candles, and bolting the door, gave me, though I expected him, some sort of alarm. He came a-tiptoe to the bedside, and saying with a gentle whisper: 'Pray, my dear, do not be startled – I will be very tender and kind to you.' He then hurried off his clothes, and leaped into bed, having given me openings enough, whilst he was stripping, to observe his brawny structure, strong-made limbs, and rough shaggy breast.

The bed shook again when it received this new load. He lay on the outside, where he kept the candles burning, no doubt for the satisfaction of every sense; for as soon as he had kissed me, he rolled down the bedclothes and seemed transported with the view of all my person at full length, which he covered with a profusion of kisses, sparing no part of me. Then, being on his knees between my thighs, he drew up his shirt and bared all his hairy thighs and stiff staring truncheon, red-topped and rooted into a thicket of curls, which covered his belly to his navel and gave it the air of a flesh-brush; and soon I felt it joining close to mine, when he had driven the nail up to the head, and left no partition but the intermediate hair on both sides.

I had it now, I felt it now, and beginning to drive, he soon gave nature such a powerful summons down to her favourite quarters that she could no longer refuse repairing thither. All my animal spirits then rushed mechanically to that center of attraction, and presently, inly warmed and stirred as I was beyond bearing, I lost all restraint, and yielding to the force of the emotion, gave down, as mere woman, those effusions of pleasure, which, in the strictness of still faithful love, I could have wished to have held up.

Yet oh! what an immense difference did I feel between this impression of a pleasure merely animal, and struck out of the collision of the sexes by a passive bodily effect, from that sweet fury, that rage of active delight which crowns the enjoyments of a mutual love-passion, where two hearts, tenderly and truly united, club to exalt the joy, and give it a spirit and soul that bids defiance to that end which mere momentary desires generally terminate in, when they die of a surfeit of satisfaction.

Mr H – , whom no distinctions of that sort seemed to distract, scarce gave himself or me breathing time from the last encounter, but as if he had tasked himself to prove that the appearances of his vigour were not signs hung out in vain, in a few minutes he was in a condition for renewing the onset, to which, preluding with a storm of kisses, he drove the same course as before with unbated fervour, and thus, in repeated engagements, kept me constantly in exercise till dawn of morning, in all which time he made me fully sensible of the virtues of his firm texture of limbs, his square shoulders, broad chest, compact hard muscles, in short, a system of manliness that might pass for no bad image of our ancient sturdy barons, when they wielded the battle-ax, whose race is now so thoroughly refined and frittered away into the more delicate modern-built frame of our pap-nerved softlings, who are as pale, as pretty, and almost as masculine as their sisters.

Mr H – , content, however, with having the day break upon his triumphs, resigned me up to the refreshment of a rest we both wanted, and we soon dropped into a profound sleep.

Though he was some time awake before me, yet did he not offer to disturb a respose he had given me so much occasion for; but on my first stirring, which was not till past ten o'clock, I was obliged to endure one more trial of his manhood.

About eleven, in came Mrs Jones, with two basins of the richest soup, which her experience in these matters had moved her to prepare. I pass over the fulsome compliments, the cant of this decent procuress, with which she saluted us both, but though my blood rose at the sight of her, I suppressed my emotions, and gave all my concern to reflections on what would be the consequence of this new engagement.

But Mr H – , who penetrated my uneasiness, did not long suffer me to languish under it and acquainted me that, having taken a solid sincere affection to me, he would begin by giving me one leading mark of it, in removing me out of a house which must for many reasons be irksome and disagreeable to me, into convenient lodgings, where he would take all imaginable care of me; and desiring me not to have any explanations with my landlady, or be impatient till he returned, he dressed and went out, having left me a purse with two and twenty guineas in it, being all he had about him as he expressed it, to keep my pocket till farther supplies.

As soon as he was gone, I felt the usual consequences of the first launch into vice; (for my love attachment to Charles never appeared to me in that light). I was instantly borne away down the stream, without the power of making back to the shore. My dreadful necessities, my gratitude, and above all, to say the plain truth, the dissipation and diversion I began to find in this new acquaintance, from the black corroding thoughts my heart had been a prey to ever since the absence of my dear Charles, concurred to stun all contrary reflections. If I now thought of my first, my only charmer, it was still with the tenderness and regret of the fondest love, embittered with the consciousness that I was no longer worthy of him. I could have begged my bread with him all over the world, but wretch that I was! I had neither the virtue or courage requisite not to outlive my separation from him.

Yet! had not my heart been thus pre-engaged, Mr H – might probably have been the sole master of it, but the place was full, and the force of conjunctures alone had made him the possessor of my person, the charms of which had, by the by, been his sole object and passion, and were, of course, no foundation for a love either very deliberate or very durable. He did not return till six in the evening to take me away to my new lodgings, and my moveables being soon packed and conveyed into a hackney-coach, it cost me but little regret to take my leave of a landlady whom I thought I had so much reason not to be overpleased with, and as for her part, she made no other difference of my staying or going but what that of the profit created.

We soon got to the house appointed for me, which was that of a plain tradesman, who, on the score of interest, was entirely at Mr H – 's devotion, and who let him the first floor, very genteelly furnished, for two guineas a week, of which I was instated mistress, with a maid to attend me.

He staid with me that evening, and we had a supper from a neighbouring tavern, after which, and a gay glass or two, the maid put me to bed. Mr H – soon followed, and, notwithstanding the fatigues of the preceding night, I found no quarter nor remission from him: he piqued himself, as he told me, on doing the honours of my new apartment.

The morning being pretty well advanced, we got to breakfast: and the ice now broke, my heart, no longer engrossed by love, began to take ease, and to please itself with such trifles as Mr H – 's liberal liking led him to make his court to the usual vanity of our sex. Silks, laces, earrings, pearl-necklace, gold watch, in short, all the trinkets and articles of dress were lavishly heaped upon me, the sense of which, if it did not create returns of love, forced a kind of grateful fondness something like love, a distinction it would be spoiling the pleasure of nine tenths of the keepers in the town to make, and is, I suppose, the very good reason why so few of them ever do make it.

I was now established the kept mistress in form, well lodged, with a very sufficient allowance and lighted up with all the lustre of dress.

Mr H – continued kind and tender to me, yet, with all this I was far from happy; for, besides my regrets for my dear youth, which, though often suspended or diverted, still returned upon me in certain melancholic moments with redoubled violence, I wanted more society, more dissipation.

As to Mr H – , he was so much my superior in every sense that I felt it too much to the disadvantage of the gratitude I owed him; thus he gained my esteem, though he could not raise my taste. I was qualified for no sort of conversation with him, except one sort, and that is a satisfaction which leaves tiresome intervals, if not filled up by love or other amusements.

Mr H – , so experienced, so learned in the ways of women, numbers of whom had passed through his hands, doubtless soon perceived this uneasiness, and without approving or liking me the better for it, had the complaisance to indulge me.

He made suppers at my lodgings, where he brought several companions of his pleasures with their mistresses, and by this means I got into a circle of acquaintance that soon stripped me of all the remains of bashfulness and modesty which might be yet left of my country education, and were, to a just

Philip Mercier: Damon and Sylvia

taste, perhaps, the greatest of my charms.

We visited one another in form, and mimicked, as near as we could, all the miseries, the follies, and impertinences of the women of quality, in the round of which they trifle away their time, without its ever entering into their little heads that on earth there cannot subsist anything more silly, more flat, more insipid and worthless than, generally considered, their system of life is: they ought to treat the men as their tyrants indeed! were they to condemn them to it.

Unknown: The Couch of Adultery (*detail*)

But though, amongst the kept mistresses (and I was now acquainted with a good many, besides some useful matrons, who live by their connexions with them) I hardly knew one that did not perfectly detest their keepers, and, of course, made little or no scruple of any infidelity they could safely accomplish. I had still no notion of wronging mine: for, besides that no mark of jealousy on his side started me the hint, or gave me the provocation to play him a trick of that sort, and that his constant generosity, politeness, and tender attentions to please me forced a regard to him, that, without affecting my heart, insured him my fidelity, no object had yet presented that could overcome the habitual liking I had contracted for him. I was on the eve of obtaining from the movements of his own voluntary generosity a modest provision for life, when an accident happened which broke all the measures he had resolved upon in my favour.

I had now lived near seven months with Mr H – , when one day returning to my lodgings from a visit in the neighbourhood, where I used to stay longer, I found the street-door open, and the maid of the house standing at it talking with some of her acquaintance, so that I came in without knocking; and as I passed by, she told me Mr H – was above. I stepped upstairs into my own bedchamber, with no other thought than pulling off my hat, etc., and then to wait upon him in the dining room, into which my bedchamber had a door, as is common enough. Whilst I was untying my hat-strings, I fancied I heard my maid Hannah's voice, and a sort of tussle, which raising my curiosity, I stole softly to the door, where a knot in the wood had been slipped out and afforded a very commanding peep-hole to the scene then in agitation, the actors of which had been too earnestly employed to hear my opening my own door, from the landing place of the stairs into my bedchamber.

The first sight that struck me was Mr H – pulling and hauling this coarse country strammel towards a couch that stood in the corner of the dining room; to which the girl made only a sort of an awkward hoydening resistance, crying out so loud that I, who listened at the door, could scarce hear her, 'Pray, Sir, don't – let me alone – I am not for your turn – You cannot, sure demean yourself with such a poor body as I –. Lord, Sir, my mistress may come home – I must not indeed. I will cry out –' All which did not hinder her from insensibly suffering herself to be brought to the foot of the couch, upon which a push of no mighty violence served to give her a very easy fall, and my gentleman having got up his hands to the stronghold of her *vartue*, she no doubt thought it was time to give up the argument, and that all further defence would be vain: and he, throwing her petticoats over her face, which was now as red as scarlet, discovered a pair of stout, plump, substantial thighs, and tolerably white; he mounted them round his hips, and coming out with his drawn weapon, stuck it in the cloven spot, where he seemed to find a less difficult entrance than perhaps he had flattered himself with (for by the way this blowze had left her place in the country for a bastard), and, indeed, all his motions showed he was lodged pretty much at large. After he had done, his dearee gets up, drops her petticoats down, and smoothes her apron and handkerchief. Mr H – looked a little silly, and taking out some money, gave it her, with an air indifferent enough, bidding her be a good girl and say nothing.

Had I loved this man, it was not in nature for me to have had patience to see the whole scene through: I should have broken in and played the jealous princess with a vengeance; but that was not the case, my pride alone was hurt, my heart not, and I could easier win upon myself to see how far he would go, till I had no uncertainty upon my conscience.

The least delicate of all affairs of this sort being now over, I retired softly into my closet, where I began to consider what I should do: my first scheme naturally was to rush in and upbraid them; this indeed flattered my present emotions and vexations, as it would have given immediate vent to them; but on second thoughts, not being so clear as to the consequence to be apprehended from such a step, I began to doubt whether it was not better to dissemble my discovery till a safer season, when Mr H – should have perfected the settlement he had made overtures to me of, and which I was not to think such a violent explanation, as I was indeed not equal to the management of, could possibly forward, and might destroy. On the other hand, the provocation seemed too gross, too flagrant, not to give me some thoughts of revenge, the very start of which idea restored me to perfect composure, and delighted as I was with the confused plan of it in my head, I was easily mistress enough of myself to support the part of ignorance I had prescribed to myself; and as all this circle of reflections was instantly over, I stole a-tiptoe to the passage-door, and opening it with a noise, passed for having that moment come home; and after a short pause, as if to pull off my things, I opened the door into the dining room, where I found the dowdy blowing the fire, and my faithful shepherd walking about the room and whistling, as cool and unconcerned as if nothing had happened. I think, however, he had not much to brag of having out-dissembled me; for I kept up, nobly, the character of our sex for art, and went up to him with the same open air of frankness as I had ever received him. He staid but a little while, made some excuse for not being able to stay the evening with me, and went out.

As for the wench, she was now spoiled, at least for my servant; and scarce eight and forty hours were gone round, before her insolence, on what had passed between Mr H – and her, gave me so fair an occasion to turn her away at a minute's warning that not to have done it would have been the wonder; so that he could neither disapprove it nor find in it the least reason to suspect my original motive. What became of her afterwards I know not; but generous as Mr H – was, he undoubtedly made her amends: though I dare answer, that

Henry Horland: A Lady's Maid Soaping Linen

he kept up no farther commerce with her of that sort, as his stooping to such a coarse morsel was only a sudden sally of lust, on seeing a wholesome-looking, buxom country wench, and no more strange than hunger, or even a whimsical appetite's making a flying meal of neck-beef, for a change of diet.

Had I considered this escape of Mr H – in no more than that light and contented myself with turning away the wench, I had thought and acted right, but, flushed as I was with imaginary wrongs, I should have held Mr H – to have been too cheaply off, if I had not pushed my revenge farther and repaid him, as exactly as I could for the soul of me, in the same coin.

Nor was this worthy act of justice long delayed: I had it too much at heart Mr H – had about a fortnight before taken into his service a tenant's son just come out of the country, a very handsome young lad scarce turned of nineteen, fresh as a rose, well shaped and clever-limbed in short, a very good excuse for any woman's liking, even though revenge had been out of the question; any woman, I say, who was disprejudiced and had wit and spirit enough to prefer a point of pleasure to a point of pride.

Mr H – had clapped a livery upon him; and his chief employ was, after being shown my lodgings, to bring and carry letters or messages between his master and me; and as the situation of all kept ladies is not the fittest to inspire respect even to the meanest of mankind, and perhaps less of it from the most ignorant, I could not help observing that this lad, who was, I suppose, acquainted with my relation to his master by his fellow servants, used to eye me in that bashful confused way, more expressive, more moving, and readier caught at by our sex than any other declarations whatever: my figure had, it seems, struck him, and modest and innocent as he was, he did not himself know that the pleasure he took in looking at me was love, or desire; but his eyes, naturally wanton, and now inflamed by passion, spoke a great deal more than he durst have imagined they did. Hitherto, indeed, I had only taken notice of the comeliness of the youth, but without the least design. My pride alone would have guarded me from a thought that way had not Mr H – 's condescension with my maid, where there was not half the temptation in point of person, set me a dangerous example; but now I began to look on this stripling as every way as delicious instrument of my designed retaliation upon Mr H – , of an obligation for which I should have made a conscience to die in his debt.

In order then to pave the way for the accomplishment of my scheme, for two or three times that the young fellow came to me with messages, I managed so as without affectation to have him admitted to my bedside or brought to me at my toilet, where I was dressing; and by carelessly showing or letting him see as if without meaning or design, sometimes my bosom rather more bare than it should be; sometimes my hair, of which I had a very fine head in the natural flow of it while combing, sometimes a neat leg that had unfortunately slipped its garter, which I made no scruple of tying before him, easily gave him the impressions favourable to my purpose which I could perceive to sparkle in his eyes and glow in his cheeks. Then certain slight squeezes by the hand, as I took letters from him did his business completely.

When I saw him thus moved and fired for my purpose, I inflamed him yet more by asking him several leading questions, such as had he a mistress? – was she prettier than me? – could he love such a one as I was? – and the like; to all which the blushing simpleton answered to my wish, in a strain of perfect undebauched innocence, but with all the awkwardness and simplicity of country breeding.

When I thought I had sufficiently ripened him for the laudable point I had in view, one day that I expected him at a particular hour, I took care to have the coast clear for the reception I designed him. And, as I had laid it, he came to the dining room door, tapped at it, and, on my bidding him come in, he did so and shut the door after him. I desired him then to bolt it on the inside, pretending it would not otherwise keep shut.

It was then lying at length on that very couch, the scene of Mr H – 's polite joys, in an undress which was with all the art of negligence flowing loose, and in a most tempting disorder: no stays, no hoop – no encumbrance whatever; on the other hand, he stood at a little distance that gave me a full view of a fine featured, shapely, healthy, country lad, breathing the sweets of fresh blooming youth: his hair, which was of a perfect shining black, played to his face in natural side-curls and was set out with a smart tuck-up behind; new buckskin breeches that, clipping close, showed the shape of a plump well made thigh, white stockings, garter-laced livery, shoulder-knot, altogether composed a figure in which the beauties of pure flesh and blood appeared under no disgrace from the lowness of a dress, to which a certain spruce neatness seems peculiarly fitted.

I bid him come towards me and give me his letter, at the same time throwing down carelessly a book I had in my hands. He coloured, and came within reach of delivering me the letter, which he held out awkwardly enough for me to take, with his eyes riveted on my bosom, which was, through the designed disorder of my handkerchief, sufficiently bare and rather shaded than hidden.

I, smiling in his face, took the letter, and immediately catching gently hold of his shirt-sleeve, drew him towards me, blushing and almost trembling; for surely his extreme bashfulness and utter inexperience called for at least all these advances to encourage him. His body was now conveniently inclined towards me, and just softly chucking his smooth beardless chin, I asked him, if he was afraid of a lady? – and with that taking and carrying his hand to my breasts, I pressed it tenderly to them. They were now finely furnished and raised in flesh, so that, panting with desire, they rose and fell, in quick heaves, under his touch: at this, the boy's eyes began to lighten with all the fires of inflamed nature, and his cheeks flushed with a deep scarlet; tongue-tied with joy, rapture, and bashfulness, he could not speak, but then his looks, his emotion, sufficiently satisfied me that my train had taken, and that I had no disappointment to fear.

My lips, which I threw in his way, so as that he could not escape kissing them, fixed, fired and emboldened him, and now, glancing my eyes towards that part of his dress which covered the essential object of enjoyment, I plainly discovered the swell and commotion there, and as I was now too far advanced to stop in so fair a way, and was indeed no longer able to contain myself or wait the slower progress of his maiden bashfulness (for such it seemed, and really was), I stole my hand upon his thighs, down one of which I could both see and feel a stiff hard body, confined by his breeches, and that my fingers could discover no end to. Curious then, and eager to unfold so alarming a mystery, playing, as it were, with his buttons, which were bursting ripe from the active force within, those of his waistband and foreflap flew open at a touch, when out it started; and now, disengaged from the shirt, I saw with wonder and surprise, what? not the plaything of a boy, not the weapon of a man, but a maypole of so enormous a standard that, had proportions been observed, it must have belonged to a young giant; its prodigious size made me shrink again. Yet I could not, without pleasure, behold and even ventured to feel such a length! such a breadth of animated ivory, perfectly well turned and fashioned, the proud stiffness of which distended its skin, whose smooth polish and velvet softness might vie with that of the most delicate of our sex, and whose exquisite whiteness was not a little set off by a sprout of black curling hair round the root, through the jetty sprigs of which the fair skin showed as, in a fine evening, you may have

Thomas Rowlandson: The Wanton Frolic

remarked the clear light ether, through the branchwork of distant trees, overtopping the summit of a hill. Then the broad and bluish-casted incarnate of the head and blue serpentines of its veins altogether composed the most striking assemblage of figure and colours in nature; in short, it stood an object of terror and delight.

But what was yet more surprising, the owner of this natural curiosity (through the want of occasions in the strictness of his home breeding, and the little time he had been in town not having afforded him one) was hitherto an absolute stranger, in practice at least, to the use of all that manhood he was so nobly stocked with; and it now fell to my lot to stand his first trial of it, if I could resolve to run the risks of its disproportion to that tender part of me which such an over-sized machine was very fit to lay in ruins.

But it was now of the latest to deliberate; for by this time, the young fellow, overheated with the present objects, and too high-mettled to be longer curbed in by that modesty and awe which had hitherto restrained him, ventured, under the stronger impulse and instructive promptership of nature alone, to slip his hands, trembling with eager impetuous desires, under my petticoats, and seeing, I suppose, nothing extremely severe in my looks to stop, or dash him, he feels out and seizes gently the center-spot of his ardours. Oh then! the fiery touch of his fingers determines me, and my fears melting away before the growing intolerable heat, my thighs disclose of themselves and yield all liberty to his hand; and now, a favourable movement giving my petticoats a toss, the avenue lay too fair, too open to be missed; he is now upon me. I had placed myself with a jet under him, as commodious and open as possible to his attempts, which were untoward enough, for his machine, meeting with no inlet, bore and battered stiffly against me in random pushes, now above, now below, now beside its point, till, burning with impatience from its irritating touches, I guided gently with my hand this furious fescue to where my young novice was now to be taught his first lesson of pleasure. Thus he nicked at length the warm and insufficient orifice; but he was made to find no breach practicable, and mine, though so often entered, was still far from wide enough to take him easily in.

By my direction, however, the head of his unwieldy machine was so critically pointed that, feeling him foreright against the tender opening, a favourable motion from me met his timely thrust, by which the lips of it, strenuously dilated, gave way to his thus assisted impetuosity, so that we might both feel that he had gained a lodgement; pursuing then his point, he soon, by violent and, to me, most painful piercing thrusts, wedges himself as least so far in as to be now tolerably secure of his entrance: here he stuck; and I now felt such a mixture of pleasure and pain as there is no giving a definition of. I dreaded, alike, his splitting me farther up or his withdrawing: I could not bear either to keep or part with him; the sense of pain, however, prevailing, from his prodigious size and stiffness, acting upon me in those continued rapid thrusts with which he furiously pursued his penetration, made me cry out gently: 'Oh, my dear, you hurt me!' This was enough to check the tender respectful boy, even in his mid-career; and he immediately drew out the sweet cause of my complaint, whilst his eyes eloquently expressed at once his grief for hurting me and his reluctance at dislodging from quarters of which the warmth and closeness had given him a gust of pleasure that he was now desire-mad to satisfy, and yet too much a novice not to be afraid of my withholding his relief, on account of the pain he had put me to.

But I was myself far from being pleased with his having too much regarded my tender exclaims, for now more and more fired with the object before me, as it still stood with the fiercest erection, unbonneted and displaying its broad vermillion head, I first gave the youth a re-encouraging kiss, which he repaid me with a fervour that seemed at once to thank me and bribe my farther compliance, and I soon replaced myself in a posture to receive, at all risks, the renewed invasion, which he did not delay an instant; for, being presently remounted, I once more felt the smooth hard gristle forcing an entrance, which he achieved rather easier than before. Pained, however, as I was, with his efforts of gaining a complete admission, which he was so regardful as to manage by gentle degrees, I took care not to complain. In the meantime the soft strait passage gradually loosens, yields, and, stretched to its utmost bearing by the stiff, thick, in-driven engine, sensible at once to the ravishing pleasure of the feel and the pain of the distension, let him in about half way, when all the most nervous activity he now exerted to further his penetration gained him not an inch of his purpose; for, whilst he hesitated there, the crisis of pleasure overtook him, and the close compressure of the warm surrounding fold drew from him the ecstatic gush, even before mine was ready to meet it, kept up by the pain I had endured in the course of the engagement, from the unsufferable size of his weapon, though it was not as yet in above half its length.

I expected then, but without wishing it, that he would draw, but was pleasingly disappointed; for he was not to be let off so. The well-breathed

Jean-Honoré Fragonard: The Happy Lovers

youth, hot-mettled, and flush with genial juices, was now fairly in for making me know my driver. As soon, then, as he had made a short pause, waking, as it were, out of the trance of pleasure (in which every sense seemed lost for a while, whilst, with his eyes shut and short quick breathings, he had yielded down his maiden tribute), he still kept his post, yet unsated with enjoyment, and solacing in these so new delights till his stiffness, which had scarce perceptibly remitted, being thoroughly recovered to him, who had not once unsheathed, he proceeded afresh to cleave and open to himself an entire entry into me, which was not a little made easy to him by the balsamic injection with which he had just plentifully moistened the whole internals of the passage. Redoubling, then, the active energy of his thrusts, favoured by the fervid appetency of my motions, the soft oiled wards can no longer stand so effectual a picklock, but yield and open him an entrance; and now, with conspiring nature and my industry, strong to aid him, he pierces, penetrates, and at length, winning his way inch by inch, gets entirely in, and finally, a home-made thrust, sheathes it up to the guard; on the information of which, from the close jointure of our bodies (insomuch that the hair on both sides perfectly interweaved and encurled together), the eyes of the transported youth sparkled with more joyous fires, and all his looks and motions acknowledged excess of pleasure, which I now began to share, for I felt him in my very vitals! I was quite sick with delight! stirred beyond bearing with its furious agitations within me, and gorged and crammed even to a surfeit: thus I lay gasping, panting, under him, till his broken breathings, faltering accents, eyes twinkling with humid fires, lunges more furious, and an increased stiffness gave me to hail the approaches of the second period: – it came – and the sweet youth, overpowered with ecstasy, died away in my arms, melting in a flood that shot in genial warmth into the innermost recesses of my body, every conduit of which, dedicated to that pleasure, was on flow to mix with it. Thus we continued for some instants, lost, breathless, senseless of everything and in every part but those favourite ones of nature, in which all that we enjoyed of life and sensation was now totally concentered.

When our mutual trance was a little over, and the young fellow had withdrawn that delicious stretcher with which he had most plentifully drowned all thoughts of revenge in the sense of actual pleasure, the widened wounded passage refunded a stream of pearly liquids, which flowed down my thighs, mixed with streaks of blood, the marks of the ravage of that montstrous machine of his, which had now triumphed over a kind of second maidenhead. I stole, however, my handkerchief to those parts and wiped them as dry as I could, whilst he was readjusting, and buttoning up.

I made him now sit down by me, and as he had gathered courage from such extreme intimacy, he gave me an aftercourse of pleasure, in a natural burst of tender gratitude and joy, at the new scenes of bliss I had opened to him; scenes positively so new that he had never before had the least acquaintance with that mysterious mark, the cloven stamp of female distinction, though nobody better qualified than he to penetrate into its deepest recesses or do it nobler justice. But when, by certain motions, certain unquietnesses of his hands, that wandered not without design, I found he languished for satisfying a curiosity natural enough, to view and handle those parts which attract and concenter the warmest force of imagination, charmed as I was to have any occasion of obliging and humouring his young desires, I suffered him to proceed as he pleased, without check or control, to the satisfaction of them.

Easily, then, reading in my eyes the full permission of myself to all his wishes, he scarce pleased himself more than me, when, having insinuated his hands under my petticoat and shift, he presently removed those bars to the sight by slily lifting them upwards, under favour of a thousand kisses, which he thought, perhaps, necessary to divert my attention to what he was about. All my drapery being now rolled up to my waist, I threw myself into such a posture upon the couch as gave up to him in full view, the whole region of delight, and all the luxurious landscape round it. The transported youth devoured everything with his eyes and tried with his fingers to lay more open to his sight the secret of that dark and delicious deep: he opens the folding lips, the softness of which yielding entry to anything of a hard body, close round it, and oppose the sight; and feeling further, meets with, and wonders at, a soft fleshy excrescence which, limber and relaxed after the late enjoyment, now grew, under the touch and examination of his fiery fingers, more and more stiff and considerable, till the titillating ardours of that so sensible part made me sigh as if he had hurt me. On which he withdrew his curious probing fingers, asking me pardon as it were, in a kiss that rather increased the flame *there*.

Novelty ever makes the strongest impressions, and in pleasures especially: no wonder then that he was swallowed up in raptures of admiration of things so interesting by their nature, and now seen and handled for the first time. On my part I was richly overpaid for the pleasure I gave him in that of examining the power of those objects thus abandoned to him, naked and free to his loosest wish, over the artless natural stripling: his eyes streaming fire, his cheeks glowing with a florid red, his fervid frequent sighs, whilst his hands convulsively squeezed, opened, pressed together again the lips and sides of that deep flesh-wound or gently twitched the over-growing moss; and all proclaimed the excess, the riot of joys, in having his wantonness thus humoured. But he did not long abuse my patience, for the objects before him had now put him by all his, and coming out with that formidable machine of his, he lets the fury loose, and pointing it directly to the pouting-lipped mouth that bid him sweet defiance in dumb-show, squeezes in the head and driving with refreshed rage, breaks in and plugs up the whole passage of that soft pleasure-conduit, where he makes all shake again, and put once more all within me into such an uproar as nothing could still but a fresh inundation from the very engine of those flames, as well as from all the springs with which nature floats that reservoir of joy, when risen to its floodmark.

I was now so bruised, so battered, so spent with this over-match that I could hardly stir or raise myself, but lay palpitating, till the ferment of my senses subsiding by degrees, and the hour striking at which I was obliged to dispatch my young man, I tenderly advised him of the necessity there was for parting, which I felt as much displeasure at as he could do, who seemed eagerly disposed to keep the field, and to enter on a fresh action; but the danger was too great, and after some hearty kisses of leave and recommendations of secrecy and discretion, I forced myself to force him away, not without assurances of seeing him again, to the same purpose, as soon as possible, and thrust a guinea into his hands: not more, lest, being too flush of money, a suspicion or discovery might arise from thence, having everything to fear from the dangerous indiscretion of that age in which young fellows would be too irresistible, too charming, if we had not that terrible fault to guard against.

Giddy and intoxicated as I was with such satiating draughts of pleasure, I still lay on the couch, supinely stretched out, in a delicious languour diffused over all my limbs, hugging myself for being thus revenged to my heart's content, and that in a manner so precisely alike, and on the identical spot, in which I had received the supposed injury. No reflections on the consequences ever once perplexed me, nor did I make myself one single reproach for having, by this step, completely entered myself of a profession more decried than disused. I should have held it in gratitude to the pleasure I had received to have repented of it; and since I was now over the bar, I thought by plunging

L. Leopold Boilly: Indiscretion

over head and ears into the stream I was hurried away by, to drown all sense of shame or reflection.

Whilst I was thus making these laudable dispositions, and whispering to myself a kind of tacit vow of incontinency, enters Mr H – . The consciousness of what I had been doing deepened yet the glowing of my cheeks, flushed with the warmth of the late action, which, joined to the piquant air of my dishabille, drew from Mr H – a compliment on my looks, which he was proceeding to back the sincerity of with proofs, and that with so brisk an action as made me tremble for fear of a discovery from the condition those parts were left in from their late severe handling: the orifice dilated and inflamed, the lips swollen with their uncommon distension, the ringlets pressed down, crushed and uncurled with the overflowing moisture that had wet everything round it, the different feel and state of things, in short, would hardly have passed, upon one of Mr H – 's nicety and experience, unaccounted for but by the real cause. But here the woman saved me: I pretended a violent disorder of my head, and feverish heat that indisposed me too much to receive his embraces. He gave in to this, and good-naturedly desisted. Soon after, an old lady coming in, made a third, very *a propos* for the confusion I was in, and Mr H – , after bidding me take care of myself and recommending me to my repose, left me much at ease and relieved by his absence.

In the close of the evening, I took care to have prepared for me a warm bath of aromatic and sweet herbs; in which, having fully laved and solaced myself, I came out voluptuously refreshed in body and spirit.

The next morning, waking pretty early after a night's perfect rest and composure, it was not without some dread and uneasiness, that I thought of what innovation that tender soft system of mine might have sustained from the shock of a machine so sized for its destruction.

Struck with this apprehension, I scarce dared to carry my hand thither, to inform myself of the state and posture of things.

But I was soon agreeably cured of my fears.

The silky hair that covered round the borders, now smoothed and repruned, had resumed its wonted curl and trimness; the fleshy pouting lips, that had stood the brunt of the engagement, were no longer swollen or moisture-drenched: and neither they nor the passage into which they opened, that had suffered so great a dilation, betrayed any the least alteration, outward or inwardly, to the most curious research, notwithstanding also the laxity that naturally follows the warm bath.

Ramsay: A Nude Woman Seen from Behind

This continuation of that grateful stricture which is in us, to the men, the very jet of their pleasure, I owed, it seems, to a happy habit of body, juicy, plump, and furnished towards the texture of those parts, with a fullness of soft springy flesh that, yielding sufficiently as it does to almost any distension, soon recovers itself so as to retighten that strict compression of its mantling and folds, which form the sides of the passage wherewith it so tenderly embraces and closely clips any foreign body introduced into it, such as my exploring finger then was.

Finding then everything in due tone and order, I remembered my fears, only to make a jest of them to myself. And now, palpably mistress of any size of man, and triumphing in my double achievement of pleasure and revenge, I abandoned myself entirely to the ideas of all the delight I had swum in. I lay stretching out, glowingly alive all over, and tossing with burning impatience of the renewal of joys that had sinned but in a sweet excess; not did I lose my longing, for about ten in the morning, according to expectation, Will, my new humble sweetheart, came with a message from his master, Mr H – , to know how I did. I had taken care to send my maid on an errand into the city, that I was sure would take up time enough; and from the people of the house I had nothing to fear, as they were plain good sort of folks, and wise enough to mind no more of other people's business than they could well help.

All dispositions then made, not forgetting that of lying in bed to receive him; when he was entered the door of my bedchamber, a latch, that I governed by a wire, descended and secured it.

I could not but observe that my young minion was as much spruced out as could be expected from one in his condition; a desire of pleasing that could not be indifferent to me, since it proved that I pleased him, which I assure you was now a point I was not above having in view.

His hair trimly dressed, clean linen, and, above all, a hale, ruddy, wholesome country look, made him out as pretty a piece of woman's meat as you should see, and I should have thought anyone much out of taste that could not have made a hearty meal of such a morsel as nature seemed to have designed for the highest diet of pleasure.

And why should I here suppress the delight I received from this amiable creature in remarking each artless look, each motion of pure undissembled nature, betrayed by his wanton eyes, or showing transparently, the glow and suffusion of blood through his fresh, clear skin, whilst even his sturdy, rustic pressures wanted not their peculiar charm? Oh! but, say you, this was a

Nicolas Lavreince: Playful Love

young fellow in too low a rank of life to deserve so great a display. May be so: but was my condition, strictly considered, one jot more exalted? Or had I really been much above him, did not his capacity of giving such exquisite pleasure sufficiently raise end ennoble him to me at last? Let who would, for me, cherish, respect, and reward the painter's, the statuary's, the musician's arts, in proportion to the delight taken in them; but at my age, and with my taste for pleasure, a taste strongly constitutional to me, the talent of pleasing, with which nature has endowed a handsome person, formed to me the greatest of all merits, compared to which the vulgar prejudices in favour of titles, dignities, honours, and the like, held a very low rank indeed! Nor, perhaps, would the beauties of the body be so much affected to be held cheap, were they in their nature to be bought and delivered; but for me, whose natural philosophy all resided in the favourite center of sense, and who was ruled by its powerful instinct in taking pleasure by its right handle, I could scarce have made a choice more to my purpose.

Mr H – 's loftier qualifications of birth, fortune, and sense laid me under a sort of subjection and constraint that were far from making harmony in the concert of love: nor had he, perhaps, thought me worth softening that superiority to; but with this lad I was more on that level which love delights in.

We may say what we please, but those we can be the easiest and freest with are ever those we like, not to say love, the best.

With this stripling, all whose art of love was the action of it, I could without check of awe or restraint, give a loose to joy and execute every scheme of dalliance my fond fancy might put me on, in which he was, in every sense, a most exquisite companion. And now my great pleasure lay in humouring all the petulances, all the wanton frolic of a raw novice just fleshed, and keen on the burning scent of his game, but unbroken to the sport: and, to carry on the figure, who could better thread the wood than he, or stand fairer for the heart of the hunt?

He advanced then to my bedside. and whilst he faltered out his message, I could observe his colour rise, and his eyes lighten with joy, in seeing me in a situation as favourable to his loosest wishes as if he had bespoke the play.

I smiled, and put out my hand towards him, which he kneeled down to (a politeness taught him by love alone, that great master of it) and greedily kissed. After exchanging a few confused questions and answers, I asked him if he would come to bed to me for the little time I could venture to detain him.

This was just asking a person dying with hunger to feast upon the dish on earth the most to his palate. Accordingly, without farther reflection, all his clothes were off in an instant; when, blushing still more at this new liberty, he got under the bedclothes I held up to receive him, and was now in bed with a woman for the first time in his life.

Here began the usual tender preliminaries, as delicious perhaps as the crowning act of enjoyment itself; which they often beget an impatience of that makes pleasure destructive of itself by hurrying on the final period, and closing that scene of bliss, in which the actors are generally too well pleased with their parts not to wish them an eternity of duration.

When we had sufficiently graduated our advances towards the main point, by toying, kissing, clipping, feeling my breasts, now round and plump, feeling that part of me I might call a furnace-mouth, from the prodigious intense heat his fiery touches had rekindled there, my young sportsman, emboldened by every freedom he could wish, wantonly takes my hand and carries it to that enormous machine of his that stood with a stiffness! a hardness! an upward bent of erection! and which, together with its bottom dependence, the inestimable bulse of lady's jewels, formed a grand show out of goods indeed! Then its dimensions, mocking either grasp or span, almost renewed my terrors. I could not conceive how, or by what means, I could take or put such a bulk out of sight. I stroked it gently, on which the mutinous rogue seemed to swell and gather a new degree of fierceness and insolence; so that finding it grew not to be trifled with any longer, I prepared for rubbers in good earnest.

Slipping then a pillow under me, that I might give him the fairest play, I guided officiously with my hand this furious battering-ram whose ruby head, presenting nearest the resemblance of a heart, I applied to its proper mark, which lay as finely elevated as we could wish, my hips being born up and my thighs at their utmost extension; the gleamy warmth that shot from it made him feel that he was at the mouth of the indraught, and driving foreright, the powerfully divided lips of that pleasure-thirsty channel received him. He hesitated a little; then, settled well in the passage, he makes his way up the straights of it, with a difficulty nothing more than pleasing, widening as he went, so as to distend and smooth each soft furrow: our pleasure increasing deliciously, in proportion as our points of mutual touch increased in that so vital part of me in which I had now taken him, all indriven and completely sheathed, and which, crammed as it was, stretched splitting ripe, gave it so gratefully straight an accommodation! so strict a fold! a suction so fierce, that gave and took unutterable delight! We had now reached the closest point of union, but when he backened to come on the fiercer, as if I had been actuated by a fear of losing him, in the height of my fury, I twisted my legs round his naked loins, the flesh of which, so firm, so springy to the touch, quivered again under the pressure; and now I had him every way encircled and begirt; and having drawn him home to me, I kept him fast there, as if I had sought to unite bodies with him at that point. This bred a pause of action, a pleasure stop; whilst that delicate glutton, my nethermouth, as full as it could hold, kept palating, with exquisite relish, the morsel that so deliciously engorged it. But nature could not long endure a pleasure that so highly provoked without satisfying it; pursuing then its darling end, the battery recommenced with redoubled exertion; nor lay I inactive on my side, but encountering him with all the impetuosity of motion I was mistress of, the downy clothing of our meeting mounts was now of real use to break the violence of the tilt, and soon, too soon indeed! the high-wrought agitation, the sweet urgency of this to-and-fro friction, raised the titillation on me to its height, so that, finding myself on the point of going, and loath to leave the tender partner of my joys behind me, I employed all the forwarding motions and arts my experience suggested to me to promote his keeping me company to our journey's end. I not only then tightened the pleasure-girth round my restless inmate by a secret spring of suction and compression that obeys the will in those parts, but stole my hand softly to that store-bag of nature's prime sweets which so pleasingly attached to its conduit-pipe from which we receive them; there feeling, and most gently indeed squeezing those tender globular reservoirs, the magic touch took instant effect, quickened and brought on upon the spur the symptoms of that sweet agony, the melting moment of dissolution, when pleasure dies by pleasure and the mysterious engine of it overcomes the titillation it has raised in those parts by plying them with the stream of warm liquid that is itself the highest of all titillations and which they thirstily express and draw in like the hot-natured leech, which, to cool itself, tenaciously attracts all the moisture within its sphere of exsuction: chiming then to me, with exquisite consent, as I melted away, his oily balsamic injection mixing deliciously with the sluices in flow from me, sheathed and blunted all the stings of pleasure, whilst it flung us into an ecstasy that extended us fainting, breathless, entranced. Thus we lay, whilst a voluptuous languor possessed and still maintained us motionless, and fast locked in one another's arms. Alas! that these delights should be no longer-lived! for now the point of pleasure, unedged by enjoyment, and all the brisk sensations flattened upon us, resigned us up to the cool cares of insipid life. Disengaging myself then from his embrace, I made him sensible of the reasons there were for his present leaving me; on which, though reluctantly, he put on his clothes with as little expedition, however, as he could help, wantonly interrupting himself between whiles with kisses, touches, and embraces, I could not refuse myself to; yet he happily returned to his master before he was missed; but at taking leave, I forced him (for he had sentiments enough to refuse it) to receive money enough to buy a silver watch, that great article of subaltern finery, which he at length accepted as a remembrance he was carefully to preserve of my affections.

And here, Madam, I ought perhaps to make you an apology for this minute detail of things that dwelt so strongly upon my memory after so deep an impression. But, besides that this intrigue bred one great revolution in my life, which historical truth requires I should not sink upon you; may I not presume that so exalted a pleasure ought not to be ungratefully forgotten or suppressed by me, because I found it in a character in low life where, by the by, it is oftener met with, purer and more unsophisticated, than amongst the false ridiculous refinements with which the great suffer themselves to be so grossly cheated by their pride: the great! than whom there exist few amongst those they call the vulgar who are more ignorant of, or who cultivate less, the art of living than they do; they, I say, who forever mistake things the most foreign to the nature of pleasure itself, whose capital favourite object is enjoyment of beauty, wherever that rare invaluable gift is found, without distinction of birth or station.

As love never had, so now revenge had no longer any share in my commerce with this handsome youth. The sole pleasures of enjoyment were now the link I held to him by: for though nature had done such great matters for him in his outward form, and especially in that superb piece of furniture she had so liberally enriched him with; though he was thus qualified to give the senses their richest feast, still there was something more wanting to create in me and constitute the passion of love. Yet Will had very good qualities, too; gentle, tractable, and, above all, grateful: silentious, even to a fault, he spoke at any time very little but made it up emphatically with action; and to do him justice, he never gave me the least reason to complain either of any tendency to encroach upon me for the liberties I allowed him or of his indiscretion in

Thomas Rowlandson: The Observers

blabbing them. There is, then, a fatality in love, or have loved him I must; for he was really a treasure, a bit for the *bonne bouche* of a duchess; and, to say the truth, my liking for him was so extreme that it was distinguishing very nicely to deny that I loved him.

My happiness, however, with him did not last long, but found an end from my own imprudent neglect. After having taken even superfluous precautions against a discovery, our success in repeated meetings emboldened me to omit the barely necessary ones. About a month after our first intercourse, one fatal morning (the season Mr H – rarely or never visited me in) I was in my closet, where my toilet stood, in nothing but my shift, a bed-gown, and under-petticoat. Will was with me, and both ever too well disposed to balk an opportunity: for my part, a warm whim, a wanton toy had just taken me, and I had challenged my man to execute it on the spot, who hesitated not to comply with my humour. I was sat in the armchair, my shift and petticoat up, my thighs wide spread and mounted over the arms of the chair, presenting the fairest mark to Will's drawn weapon, which he stood in act to plunge into me, when, having neglected to secure the chamber door, and that of the closet standing ajar, Mr H – stole in upon us, before either of us was aware, and saw us precisely in these convicting attitudes.

I gave a great scream, and dropped my petticoat: the thunderstuck lad stood trembling and pale, waiting his sentence of death. Mr H – looked somtimes at one, sometimes at the other, with a mixture of indignation and scorn, and, without saying a word, spun upon his heel and went out.

As confused as I was, I heard him very distinctly turn the key and lock the chamber door upon us, so that there was no escape but through the dining room, where he himself was walking about with distempered strides, stamping in a great chase, and doubtless debating what he should do with us.

In the meantime, poor William was frightened out of his senses, and as much need as I had of spirits to support myself, I was obliged to employ them all to keep his a little up. The misfortune I had now brought upon him endeared him the more to me, and I could have joyfully suffered any punishment he had not shared in. I watered plentifully with my tears the face of the frightened youth, who sat, not having strength to stand, as cold and as lifeless as a statue.

Presently Mr H – comes in to us again, and made us go before him into the dining room, trembling and dreading the issue. Mr H – sat down on a chair, whilst we stood like criminals under examination, and, beginning with me,

Hogarth: After

asked me with an even firm tone of voice, neither soft nor severe, but cruelly indifferent, what I could say for myself for having abused him in so unworthy a manner with his own servant, too, and how he had deserved this of me?

Without adding to the guilt of my infidelity that of an audacious defence of it, in the old style of a common kept Miss, my answer was modest and, often interrupted by my tears, in substance as follows: that I had never had a single thought of wronging him (which was true) till I had seen him taking the last liberties with my servant-wench, (here he coloured prodigiously) and that my resentment at that which I was over-awed from giving a vent to by complaints, or explanations with him, had driven me to a course that I did not pretend to justify; but that, as to the young man, he was entirely faultless, for that in the view of making him the instrument of my revenge, I had downright seduced him to what he had done, and therefore hoped, whatever he determined about me, he would distinguish between the guilty and the innocent; and, that, for the rest, I was entirely at his mercy.

Mr H – , on hearing what I said, hung his head a little; but instantly recovering himself, he said to me, as near as I can retain, to the following purpose:

'Madam, I take shame to myself and confess you have fairly turned the tables upon me, – it is not with one of your cast of breeding and sentiments that I should enter into a discussion of the very great difference of the provocations: be it sufficient that I allow you so much reason on your side as to have changed my resolutions, in consideration of what you reproach me with; and I own, too, that your clearing that rascal there is fair and honest in you; renew with you I cannot; the affront is too gross, I give you a week's warning to go out of these lodgings: whatever I have given you remains to you; and as I never intend to see you more, the landlord will pay you fifty pieces on my account, with which, and every debt paid, I hope you will own I do not leave you in a worse condition than what I took you up in, or than you deserve of me. - Blame yourself only that it is no better.'

Then, without giving me time to reply, he addressed himself to the young fellow.

'For you, spark, I shall for your father's sake take care of you: the town is no place for such an easy fool as thou art; and tomorrow you shall set out under the charge of one of my men, well recommended, in my name, to your father, not to let you return and be spoiled here.'

At these words he went out, after my vainly attempting to stop him by throwing myself at his feet: he took me off, though he seemed greatly moved, too, and took Will away with him, who, I dare swear, thought himself very cheaply off.

P. Sandby: A Windsor Character

I was now once more adrift, and left upon my own hands by a gentleman whom I certainly did not deserve. And all the letters, arts, friends' entreaties that I employed within the week of grace in my lodging could never win on him so much as to see me again. He had irrevocably pronounced my doom, and submission to it was my only part. Soon after, he married a lady of birth and fortune, to whom I have heard he proved an irreproachable husband.

As for poor Will, he was immediately sent down to the country, to his father, who was an easy farmer, where he was not four months before an innkeeper's buxom young widow, with a very good stock both in money and trade, fancied and, perhaps pre-acquainted with his secret excellencies, married him; and I am sure there was at least one good foundation for their living happily together.

Though I should have been charmed to see him before he went, such measures were taken by Mr H – 's orders that it was impossible; otherwise I should certainly have endeavoured to detain him in town, and would have spared neither offers nor expense to have procured myself the satisfaction of keeping him with me: he had such powerful holds upon my inclinations as were not easily to be shaken off or replaced; as to my heart, it was quite out of the question; glad, however, I was from my soul that nothing worse, and, as things turned out, probably nothing better, could have happened to him.

As to Mr H–, though views of conveniency made me at first exert myself to regain his affection, I was giddy and thoughtless enough to be much easier reconciled to my failure than I ought to have been; but as I never had loved him, and his leaving me gave me a sort of liberty that I have often longed for, I was soon comforted; and flattering myself that the stock of youth and beauty

Rowlandson: Box-Lobby Loungers (*detail*)

I was going into trade with could hardly fail of procuring me a maintenance, I saw myself under a necessity of trying my fortune with them, rather with pleasure and gaiety than with the least idea of despondence.

In the meantime, several of my acquaintance amongst the sisterhood, who had soon got wind of my misfortune, flocked to insult me with their malicious consolations: most of them had long envied me the affluence and splendour I had been maintained in; and though there was scarce one of them that did not at least deserve to be in my case, and would probably sooner or later come to it, it was equally easy to remark, even in their affected pity, their secret pleasure at seeing me thus disgraced and discarded, and their secret grief that it was still no worse with me. Unaccountable malice of the human heart! and which is not confined to the class of life they were of.

But as the time approached for me to come to some resolution how to dispose of myself, and I was considering round where to shift my quarters to, Mrs Cole, a middle-aged discreet sort of woman, who had been brought into my acquaintance by one of the misses that visited me, upon learning my situation, came to offer her cordial advice and service to me; and as I had always taken to her more than to any of my female acquaintance, I listened the easier to her proposals: and as it happened, I could not have put myself into worse or into better hands in all London: into worse, because keeping a house of conveniency, there were no lengths in lewdness she would not advise me to go, in compliance with her customers, no schemes of pleasure, or even unbounded debauchery, she did not take even a delight in promoting; into better, because nobody having had more experience of the wicked part of the town than she had, was fitter to advise and guard one against the worst dangers of our profession; and what was rare to be met with in those of hers, she contented herself with a moderate living profit upon her industry and good offices and had nothing of their greedy rapacious turn. She was really too a gentlewoman born and bred, but through a train of accidents reduced to this course, which she pursued: partly through necessity, partly through choice, as never woman delighted more in encouraging a brisk circulation of the trade, for the sake of the trade itself, or better understood all the mysteries and refinements of it than she did; so that she was consummately at the top of her profession, and dealt only with customers of distinction; to answer the demands of whom she kept a competent number of her daughters in constant recruit: so she called those whom their youth and personal charms recommended to her adoption and management, several of whom, by her means and through her tuition and instructions, succeeded very well in the world.

This useful gentlewoman, upon whose protection I now threw myself, having her reasons of state, respecting Mr H –, for not appearing too much in the thing herself, sent a friend of hers, on the day appointed for my removal, to conduct me to my new lodgings at a brush-makers in R – street, Covent-Garden, the very next door to her own house, where she had no conveniences to lodge me herself; lodgings that, by having been for several successions tenanted by ladies of pleasure, the landlord of them was familiarized to their ways; and provided the rent was duly paid, everything else was as easy and as commodious as one could desire.

The fifty guineas promised me by Mr H – , at his parting with me, having been duly paid me, all my clothes and movables chested up, which were at least of two hundred pounds' value, I had them conveyed into the coach, where I soon followed them, after taking a civil leave of the landlord and his family, with whom I had never lived in a degree of familiarity enough to regret the removal; but still, the very circumstance of its being a removal drew tears from me. I left, too, a letter of thanks for Mr H – , from whom I concluded myself, as I really was, irretrievably separated.

My maid I had discharged the day before, not only because I had her of Mr H – , but that I suspected her of having somehow or other been the occasion of his discovering me, in revenge, perhaps, for my not having trusted her in it.

We were soon got to my lodgings, which, though not so handsomely furnished nor so showy as those I left, were to the full as convenient, and at half price, though on the first floor. My trunks were safely landed and stowed in my apartments, where my neighbour and now governante, Mrs Cole, was ready with my landlord to receive me, to whom she took care to set me out in the most favourable light, that of one from whom there was the clearest reason to expect the regular payment of his rent: all the cardinal virtues attributed to me would not have had half the weight of that recommendation alone.

I was now settled in lodgings of my own, abandoned to my own conduct, and turned loose upon the town, to sink or swim, as I could manage with the current of it: and what were the consequences, together with the number of adventures which befell me in the exercise of my new profession, will compose the matter of another letter; for, surely, it is high time to put a period to this.

I am,
MADAM
Yours, &c. &c. &c.

Part Two

Madam,

If I have delayed the sequel of my history, it has been purely to afford myself a little breathing time, not without some hopes that, instead of pressing me to a continuation, you would have acquitted me of the task of pursuing a confession, in the course of which my self-esteem has so many wounds to sustain.

I imagined, indeed, that you would have been cloyed and tired with the uniformity of adventures and expressions, inseparable from a subject of this sort, whose bottom or groundwork being, in the nature of things, eternally one and the same, whatever variety of forms and modes the situations are susceptible of, there is no escaping a repetition of near the same images, the same figures, the same expressions, with this further inconvenience added to the disgust it creates that the words *joys, ardours, transports, ecstasies*, and the rest of those pathetic terms so congenial to, so received in the *practice of pleasure*, flatten and lose much of their due spirit and energy by the frequency they indispensibly recur with, in a narrative of which that *practice* professedly composes the whole basis. I must therefore trust to the candour of your judgment for your allowing for the disadvantage I am necessarily under in that respect, and to your imagination and sensibility the pleasing task of repairing it by their supplements, where my descriptions flag or fail: the one will readily place the pictures I present before your eyes; the other give life to the colours where they are dull, or worn with too frequent handling.

What you say besides, by way of encouragement, concerning the extreme difficulty of continuing so long in one strain, in a mean tempered with taste, between the revoltingness of gross, rank, and vulgar expressions, and the ridicule of mincing metaphors and affected circumlocutions, is so sensible as well as good-natured that you greatly justify me to myself for my compliance with a curiosity that is to be satisfied so extremely at my expense.

Resuming now where I broke off in my last I am in my way to remark to you that it was late in the evening before I arrived at my new lodgings, and

Hogarth: Night (*detail*)

Mrs Cole, after helping me to range and secure my things, spent the whole evening with me in my apartment, where we supped together, in giving me the best advice and instruction with regard to this new stage of my profession I was now to enter upon, and passing thus from a private devotee to pleasure into a public one, to become a more general good, with all the advantages requisite to put my person out to use, either for interest or pleasure, or both. But then she observed, as I was a kind of new face upon the town, that it was an established rule, and mystery of the trade, for me to pass for a maid and dispose of myself as such on the first good occasion, without prejudice, however, to such diversions as I might have a mind to the interim: for that nobody could be a greater enemy than she was to the losing of time. That she would, in the meantime, do her best to find out a proper person, and would undertake to manage this nice point for me, if I would accept of her aid and advice to such good purpose that, in the loss of a fictitious maidenhead, I should reap all the advantages of a native one.

As a great delicacy of sentiments did not extremely belong to my character at that time, I confess against myself that I perhaps too readily closed with a proposal which my candour and ingenuity gave me some repugnance to: but not enough to contradict the intention of one to whom I had now thoroughly abandoned the direction of all my steps. For Mrs Cole had, I do not know how, unless by one of those unaccountable invincible sympathies that nevertheless form the strongest links, especially of female friendship, won and got entire possession of me. On her side, she pretended that a strict resemblance she fancied she saw in me to an only daughter, whom she had lost at my age, was the first motive of her taking to me so affectionately as she did; it might be so: there exist as slender motives of attachments that gathering force from habit and liking, have proved often more solid and durable than those founded on much stronger reasons: but this I know, that, though I had had no other acquaintance with her than seeing her at my lodgings when I lived with Mr H – , where she had made errands to sell me some millinery ware, she had by degrees insinuated herself so far into my confidence that I threw myself blindly into her hands and came, at length, to regard, love, and obey her implicitly; and, to do her justice, I never experienced at her hands other than a sincerity of tenderness and care for my interest hardly heard of in those of her profession. We parted that night, after having settled a perfect unreserved agreement; and the next morning Mrs Cole came and took me with her to her house for the first time.

Here, at the first sight of things, I found everything breathe an air of decency, modesty, and order.

In the outer parlour, or rather shop, sat three young women, very demurely employed on millinery work, which was the cover of a traffic in more precious commodities: but three beautifuller creatures could hardly be seen. Two of them were extremely fair, the eldest not above nineteen, and the third, much about that age, was a piquant brunette whose black sparkling eyes and perfect harmony of features and shapes left her nothing to envy in her fairer companions. Their dress, too, had the more design in it, the less it appeared to have, being in a taste of uniform correct neatness and elegant simplicity. These were the girls that composed the small domestic flock which my governess trained up with surprising order and management, considering the giddy wildness of young girls once got upon the loose. But then she never continued any in her house whom, after a due noviciate, she found untractable or unwilling to comply with the rules of it. Thus had she insensibly formed a little family of love, in which the members found so sensibly their account in a rare alliance of pleasure with interest, and of a necessary outward decency with unbounded secret liberty, that Mrs Cole, who had picked them as much for their temper as their beauty, governed them with use to herself and them too.

To these pupils then of hers, whom she had prepared, she presented me as a new boarder, and one that was to be immediately admitted to all the intimacies of the house; upon which these charming girls gave me all the marks of a welcome reception, and indeed of being perfectly pleased with my figure, that I could possibly expect from any of my own sex, but they had been effectually brought to sacrifice all jealousy or competition of charms to a common interest and considered me as a partner that was bringing no despicable stock of goods into the trade of the house: they gathered round me, viewed me on all sides: and, as my admission into this joyous troop made a little holiday, the show of work was laid aside, and Mrs Cole, giving me up with special recommendation, to their caresses and entertainment, went about her ordinary business of the house.

The sameness of our sex, age, profession and views soon created as unreserved a freedom and intimacy as if we had been for years acquainted. They took and showed me the house, their respective apartments, which were furnished with every article of conveniency and luxury, and, above all, a spacious drawing room where a select revelling band usually met in general parties of pleasure; the girls supping with their sparks, and acting their wanton pranks with unbounded licentiousness, whilst a defiance of awe, modesty, or jealousy were their standing rules, by which, according to the principles of their society, whatever pleasure was lost on the side of sentiment was abundantly made up to the senses in the poignancy of variety and the charms of ease and luxury. The authors and supporters of this secret institution would, in the height of their humour, style themselves the restorers of the liberty of the golden age and its simplicity of pleasures, before their

Sir Joshua Reynolds: Portrait of Kitty Fisher

innocence became so unjustly branded with the names of guilt and shame.

As soon then as the evening began, and the show of a shop was shut, the academy opened, the mask of mock-modesty was completely taken off, and all the girls delivered over to their respective calls of pleasure or interest with their men; and none of that sex were promiscuously admitted, but only such as Mrs Cole was previously satisfied of their character and discretion. In short, this was the safest, politest, and, at the same time, the most thorough house of accommodation in town, everything being conducted so that decency made no intrenchment upon the most libertine pleasures, in the practice of which, too, the choice familiars of the household found the secret so rare and difficult of reconciling even all the refinements of taste and delicacy with the most gross and determinate gratifications of sensuality.

After having consumed the morning in the endearments and instructions of my new acquaintance, we went to dinner, when Mrs Cole, presiding at the head of her cluck, gave me the first idea of her management and address, in inspiring these lively amiable girls with so sensible a love and respect for her. There was no stiffness, no reserve, no airs of pique, or little jealousies, but all was unaffectedly gay, cheerful, and easy.

After dinner, Mrs Cole, seconded by the young ladies, acquainted me that there was a chapter to be held that night in form, for the ceremony of my reception into the sisterhood, and in which, with all due reserve to my maidenhead that was to be occasionally cooked up for the first proper chapman, I was to undergo a ceremonial of initiation they were sure I should not be displeased with.

Embarked as I was, and moreover captivated with the charms of my new companions, I was too much prejudiced in favour of any proposal they could make, to so much as hesitate an assent, which, therefore, readily giving, in the style of a *carte blanche*, I received fresh kisses of compliment from them all, in approval of my docility and good nature. Now I was a 'sweet girl –' I came into things 'with a good grace –' I was 'not affectedly coy –' I should be the 'pride of the house –' and the like.

This point thus adjusted, the young women left Mrs Cole to talk and concert matters with me, when she explained to me that I should be introduced that very evening to four of her best friends, one of whom she had, according to the custom of the house, favoured with the preference of engaging me in the first party of pleasure, assuring me at the same time that they were all young gentlemen agreeable in their persons, and unexceptionable in every respect; that, united and holding together by the band of common pleasures, they composed the chief support of her house, and made very liberal presents to the girl that pleased and humoured them, so that they were, properly speaking, the founders and patrons of this little seraglio. Not but that she had, at proper seasons, other customers to deal with, whom she stood less upon punctilio with than with these: for instance, it was not on one of them she could attempt to pass me for a maid; they were not only too knowing, too much town-bred to bite at such a bait, but they were such generous benefactors to her that it would be unpardonable to think of it.

Amidst all the flutter and emotion which this promise of pleasure, for such I conceived it, stirred up in me, I preserved so much of the woman as to feign just reluctance enough to make some merit of sacrificing it to the influence of my patroness, whom I likewise, still in character, reminded of it perhaps being right for me to go home and dress in favour of my first impressions.

But Mrs Cole, in opposition to this, assured me that the gentlemen I should be presented to were, by their rank and taste of things, infinitely superior to the being touched with any glare of dress or ornaments, such as silly women rather confound, and overlay, than set off their beauty with; that these veteran voluptuaries knew better than not to hold them in the highest contempt; they with whom the pure native charms alone could pass current, and who would at any time leave a sallow, washy, painted duchess on her own hands, for a ruddy, healthy, firm-fleshed country maid; and as for my part, that nature had done enough for me to set me above owing the least favour to art; concluding withal, that for the instant occasion there was no dress like an undress.

I thought my governess too good a judge of these matters not to be easily overruled by her; after which she went on preaching very pathetically the doctrine of passive obedience and nonresistance to all those arbitrary tastes of pleasure which are by some styled the refinements, and by others the deprivations of it; between whom it was not the business of a simple girl, who was to profit by pleasing, to decide, but to conform.

Over tea, Fanny is introduced to her colleagues, Emily, Harriet and Louisa, who entertain her with accounts of their own first sexual experiences.

These little histories having brought the time for the first to retire and to prepare for the revels of the evening, I staid with Mrs Cole till Emily came and told us the company was met, and waited for us.

Mrs Cole on this, taking me by the hand, with a smile of encouragement, led me upstairs, preceded by Louisa, who was come to hasten us, and lighted us with two candles, one in each hand.

On the landing place of the first pair of stairs we were met by a young gentleman, extremely well dressed, and a very pretty figure, to whom I was to be indebted for the first essay of the pleasures of the house. He saluted me with great gallantry and handed me into the drawing room, the floor of which was over-spread with a Turkey-carpet, and all its furniture voluptuously adapted to every demand of the most studied luxury. Now too it was, by means of a profuse illumination, enlivened by a light scarce inferior to, and perhaps more favourable to joy, more tenderly pleasing than that of broad sunshine.

On my entrance into the room, I had the satisfaction to hear a buzz of approbation run through the whole company, which now consisted of four gentlemen, including my particular (this was the cant term of the house for one's gallant for the time), the three young women, in a neat flowing dishabille, the mistess of the academy, and myself. I was welcomed and saluted by a kiss all round, in which, however, it was easy to discover, in the superior warmth of that of the men, the distinction of the sexes.

Awed and confounded as I was at seeing myself surrounded, caressed, and made court to by so many strangers, I could not immediately familiarize myself to all that air of gaiety and joy, which dictated their compliments and animated their caresses. They assured me that I was so perfectly their taste as to have but one fault against me, which I might easily be cured of; and that was my modesty: this, they observed, might pass for a beauty the more with those who wanted it for a heightener; but their maxim was that it was an impertinent mixture, and dashed the cup so as to spoil the sincere draught of pleasure. They considered it accordingly as their mortal enemy, and gave it no quarter wherever they met with it; this was a prologue not unworthy of the revels that ensued.

In the midst of all the frolic and wantonnesses, which this joyous band had presently and all naturally run into, an elegant supper was served in, and we sat down to it, my spark elect placing himself next to me, and the other couples without order or ceremony. The delicate cheer and good wine soon

William Hogarth: The Rake's Progress, The Orgy

Rowlandson: High Spirits

banished all reserve; the conversation grew as lively as could be wished, without taking too loose a turn. These professors of pleasure knew too well to stale the impressions of it, or evaporate the imagination in words, before the time of action. Kisses, however, were snatched at times, or where a handkerchief round the neck interposed its feeble barrier, it was not extremely respected: the hands of the men went to work with their usual petulance, till the provocations on both sides rose to such a pitch that my particular's proposal for beginning the country dances was received with instant assent: for, as he laughingly added, he fancied the instruments were in tune. This was a signal for preparations that the complaisant Mrs Cole, who understood life, took for her cue of disappearing; no longer so fit for personal service herself, and content with having settled the order of battle, she left us the field to fight it out at discretion.

As soon as she was gone, the table was removed from the middle and became a sideboard; a couch was brought into its place, of which when I whisperingly inquired the reason of my particular, he told me that as it was chiefly on my account that this convention was met, the parties intended at once to humour their taste of variety in pleasures, and by an open public enjoyment, to see me broken of any taint of reserve or modesty, which they looked on as the poison of joy; that though they occasionally preached pleasure, and lived up to the text, they did not enthusiastically set up for its missionaries, and only indulged themselves in the delights of a practical instruction of all the pretty women they liked well enough to bestow it upon, and fell properly in the way of it; but that as such a proposal might be too violent, too shocking for a young beginner, the older standers were to set an example, which he hoped I would not be adverse to follow, since it was to him I was devolved in favour of the first experiment; but that still I was perfectly at my liberty to refuse the party, which being in its nature one of pleasure, supposed an exclusion of all force or constraint.

My countenance expressed, no doubt, my surprise, as my silence did my acquiescence. I was now embarked and thoroughly determined on any voyage the company would take me on.

The first that stood up to open the ball were a cornet of horse and that sweetest of olive-beauties, the soft and amorous Louisa. He led her to the couch, 'nothing loth', on which he gave her the fall and extended her at her length with an air of roughness and vigour, relishing high of amorous eagerness and impatience. The girl, spreading herself to the best advantage, with her head upon the pillow, was so concentered in what she was about that our presence seemed the least of her cares or concern. Her petticoats, thrown up with her shift, discovered to the company the finest turned legs and thighs that could be imagined, and in a broad display that gave us a full view of that delicious cleft of flesh into which the pleasingly hair-grown mount over it parted and presented a most inviting entrance, between two close ledges, delicately soft and pouting. Her gallant was now ready, having disencumbered himself from his clothes, overloaded with lace, and presently, his shirt removed, shewed us his forces in high plight, bandied and ready for action. But giving us not time to consider dimensions, and proving the stiffness of his weapon by his impatience of delay, he threw himself instantly over his charming antagonist, who received him as he pushed at once dead at mark, like a heroine, without flinching, for surely never was a girl constitutionally truer to the taste of joy, or sincerer in the expressions of its sensations, than she was: we could observe the pleasure lighten in her eyes as he introduced his plenipotentiary instrument into her, till at length, having indulged her its utmost reach, its irritations grew so violent, and gave her the spurs so

Thomas Rowlandson: A Scene in a Farce

furiously that, collected within herself, and lost to everything but the enjoyment of her favourite feelings, she retorted his thrusts with a just concert of springy heaves, keeping time so exactly with the most pathetic sighs that one might have numbered the strokes in agitation by their distinct murmurs, whilst her active limbs kept wreathing and intertwisting with his in convulsive folds. Then the turtle-billing kisses, and the poignant painless love-bites, which they both exchanged in a rage of delight, all conspiring towards the melting period, it soon came on, when Louisa, in the ravings of her pleasure-frenzy, impotent of all restraint, cried out: 'Oh Sir! – Good Sir! – pray do not spare me! ah! ah! – I can no more.' And all her accents now faltering into heart-fetched sighs, she closed her eyes in the sweet death, in the instant of which she was deliciously embalmed by an injection, of which we could easily see the signs in the quiet, dying, languid posture of her late so furious driver, who was stopped of a sudden, breathing short, panting, and, for that time, giving up the spirit of pleasure.

As soon as he was dismounted, Louisa sprang up, shook her petticoats, and running up to me, gave me a kiss and drew me to the sideboard to which she was herself handed by her gallant, where they made me pledge them in a glass of wine, and toast a droll health of Louisa's proposal in high frolic: that of 'the miraculous thing which wets where it tickles and tickles where it wets'.

By this time the second couple was ready to enter the lists, which were a young baronet and that delicatest of charmers, the winning tender Harriet. My gentle esquire came to acquaint me with it, and brought me back to the scene of action.

And surely, never did one of her profession accompany her dispositions for the bare-faced part she was engaged to play with such a peculiar grace of sweetness, modesty, and yielding coyness, as she did. All her air and motions breathed only unreserved, unlimited complaisance, without the least mixture of impudence or prostitution. But, what was yet more surprising, her spark elect, in the midst of the dissolution of public open enjoyment, doted on her to distraction, and had, by dint of love and sentiments, touched her heart, though for a while the restraint of the engagement to the house laid him under a kind of necessity of complying with an institution which he himself had had the greatest share in establishing.

Harriet then was led to the vacant couch by her gallant, blushing as she looked at me, and with eyes made to justify anything, tenderly bespeaking of me the most favourable construction of the step she was thus irresistibly drawn into.

Her lover, for such he was, sat her down at the foot of the couch, and passing his arms round her neck, preluded with a kiss fervently applied to her lips, that visibly gave her life and spirit to go through with the scene. And as he kissed, he gently inclined his head, till it fell back on a pillow disposed to receive it, and leaning himself down all the way with her, at once countenanced and endeared her fall to her. There as if he had guessed our wishes, or meant to gratify at once his pleasure and his pride in being the master, by title of present possession. of beauties delicate beyond imagination, he discovered her breasts to his own touch and our common view. But oh! what delicious manuals of love-devotion! How inimitably fine-moulded! small, round, firm, and excellently white; then the grain of their skin, so soothing, so flattering to the touch! and their nipples, that crowned them the sweetest buds of beauty! When he had feasted his eyes with the touch and perusal, feasted his lips with kisses of the highest relish, imprinted in those all-delicious twin orbs, he proceeded downwards.

Her legs still kept the ground; and now, with the tenderest attention not to shock or alarm her too suddenly, he, by degrees, rather stole than rolled up her petticoats, at which, as if a signal had been given, Louisa and Emily took hold of her legs, in pure wantonness and yet in ease, too, to her, kept them stretched wide abroad. Then lay exposed, or, to speak more properly, displayed, the greatest parade in nature of female charms. The whole company, who, except myself, had often seen them, seemed as much dazzled, surprised, and delighted as anyone could be who had now beheld them for the first time. Beauties so excessive could not but enjoy the privileges of eternal novelty. Her thighs were so exquisitely fashioned that, either more in or more out of flesh than they were, they would have declined from that point of perfection they presented. But what infinitely enriched and adorned them was the sweet intersection formed, where they met, at the bottom of the smoothest, roundest, whitest belly, by that central furrow which nature had sunk there, between the soft relievo of two pouting ridges, and which in this girl was in perfect symmetry of delicacy and miniature with the rest of her frame. No! nothing in nature could be of a beautifuller cut. Then the dark umbrage of the downy sprig-moss that over-arched it, bestowed on the luxury of the landscape, a touching warmth, a tender finishing, beyond the expression of words or even the paint of thought.

Her truly enamoured gallant, who had stood absorbed and engrossed by the pleasure of the sight long enough to afford us time to feast ours (no fear of glutting!), addressed himself at length to the materials of enjoyment; and lifting the linen veil that hung between us and his master-member of the revels, exhibited one whose eminent size proclaimed the owner a true woman's hero. He was, besides, in every other respect an accomplished gentleman and in the bloom and vigour of youth. Standing then between Harriet's legs, which were supported by her two companions at their widest extension, with one hand he gently disclosed the lips of that luscious mouth of nature, whilst with the other, he stooped his mighty machine to its lure, from the height of its stiff stand-up towards his belly; the lips, kept open by his fingers, received its broad shelving head of coral hue; and when he had nestled it in, he hovered there a little, and the girls then delivered over to his hips the agreeable office of supporting her thighs. And now, as if he meant to spin out his pleasure and give it the more play for its life, he passed up his instrument so slow that we lost sight of it inch by inch, till at length it was wholly taken into the soft laboratory of love, and the mossy mounts of each fairly met together. In the meantime, we could plainly mark the prodigious effect the progressions of this delightful energy wrought in this delicious girl, gradually heightening her beauty as they heightened her pleasure. Her countenance, and whole frame grew more animated; the faint blush of her cheeks, gaining ground on the white, deepened into a florid vivid vermillion glow; her naturally brilliant eyes now sparkled with ten-fold lustre; her languor was vanished, and she appeared quick-spirited and alive all over. He had now fixed, nailed, this tender creature with his home-driven wedge, so that she lay passive per force, and unable to stir, till beginning to play a strain of arms against this vein of delicacy, as he urged the to-and-fro confriction, he awakened, roused,and touched her so to the heart that, unable to contain herself, she could not but reply to his motions as briskly as her nicety of frame would admit of, till the raging stings of the pleasure, rising towards the point, made her wild with the intolerable sensations of it, and she now threw her legs and arms about at random, as she lay lost in the sweet transport; which on his side again declared itself by quicker, eagerer thrusts, convulsive grasps, burning sighs, swift laborious breathings, eyes darting humid fires: all faithful tokens of the imminent approaches of the last gasp of joy. It came on at length: the baronet led the ecstasy, which she critically joined in, as she felt the melting symptoms from him, in the nick of which, glueing more ardently than ever his lips to hers, with eyes lifted up in a trance, he showed all the signs of that agony of bliss being strong upon him, in which he sent his soul, distilled in liquid sweets, up the body of that charming creature and gave her the finishing titillation; inly thrilled with which, we saw plainly that she answered it down with all the effusion of spirit and matter she was mistress of, whilst a general soft shudder ran through all her limbs, which she gave a stretch-out of, and lay motionless, breathless, dying with dear delight; and in the height of its expression showing, through the nearly closed lids of her eyes, just the edges of their black, the rest being rolled strongly upwards in her ecstasy. Then her sweet mouth appeared languishingly open, with the tip of her tongue leaning negligently towards the lower range of her white teeth, whilst the natural ruby colour of her lips glowed with heightened life. Was this a subject not to dwell upon? And accordingly her lover still kept on her with an abiding delectation, till compressed, squeezed, and distilled to the last drop, he slipped out at last and took leave with one fervent kiss, expressing satisfied desires but unextinguished love.

As soon as he was off, I ran to her, and sitting down on the couch by her, raised her head, which she declined gently and hung in my bosom, to hide her blushes and confusion at what had passed, till by degrees she recomposed herself and accepted of a restorative glass of wine from my spark, who had left me to fetch it her, whilst her own was re-adjusting his affairs and buttoning up, after which he led her, leaning languishingly upon him, to our stand of view round the couch.

And now Emily's partner had taken her out for her share in the dance, when this transcendently fair and sweet-tempered creature readily stood up: and if a complexion to put the rose and lily out of countenance, extreme pretty features, and that florid health and bloom for which the country girl are so lovely might pass her for a beauty, she certainly was one, and one of the most striking of the fair ones.

Her gallant began first, as she stood, to disengage her breasts and restore them to the liberty of nature, from the easy confinement of no more than a pair of jumps; but on their coming out to view, we thought a new light was added to the room, so superiorly shining was their whiteness; then they rose in so happy a swell as to compose her a well-formed fullness of bosom, that had such an effect on the eye as to seem flesh hardening into marble, of which it emulated the polished gloss, and far surpassed even the whitest in the life and lustre of its colours, white veined with blue. Who could refrain from such provoking enticements to it in reach? He touched her breasts first lightly when the glossy smoothness of the skin eluded his hand, and made it slip along the surface; he pressed them, and the springy flesh that filled them, thus pitted by force, rose again reboundingly with his hand and on the instant effaced the dint of the pressure: and alike indeed was the consistence of all those parts of her body throughout, where the fullness of flesh compacts and constitutes all that fine firmness which the touch is so highly attached to. When he had thus largely pleased himself with this branch of dalliance and delight, he trussed up her petticoat and shift in a wisp to her waist, where being tucked in, she stood fairly naked on every side. A blush at this

Rowlandson: The Pleasures of Convalescence

overspread her lovely face, and her eyes, downcast to the ground, seemed to beg for quarter, when she had so great a right to triumph in all the treasures of youth and beauty that she now so victoriously displayed. Her legs were perfectly well shaped, and her thighs, which she kept pretty close, showed so white, so round, so substantial, and abounding in firm flesh, that nothing could offer a stronger recommendation to the luxury of the touch, which he accordingly did not fail to indulge himself in. Then gently removing her hand, which in the first emotion of natural modesty she had carried thither, he gave us rather a glimpse than a view of that soft narrow chink, running its little length downwards and hiding the remains of it between her thighs: but plain was to be seen the fringe of light-brown curls, in beauteous growth over it, that, with their silky gloss, created a pleasing variety from the surrounding white, whose lustre, too, their gentle embrowning shade considerably raised. Her spark then endeavoured, as she stood, by disclosing her thighs, to gain us a completer sight of that central charm of attraction, but not obtaining it so conveniently in that attitude, he led her to the foot of the couch, and bringing to it one of the pillows, gently inclined her head down, so that as she leaned with it over her crossed hands, straddling with her thighs wide spread and jutting her body out, she presented a full back-view of her person, naked to her waist. Her posteriors, plump, smooth, and prominent, formed luxuriant tracts of animated snow that splendidly filled the eye, till it was commanded down the parting or separation of those exquisitely white cliffs, by their narrow vale, and was there stopped, and attracted by the embowered bottom-cavity, that terminated this delightful vista and stood modestly gaping from the influence of her bended posture, so that the agreeable interior red of the sides of the orifice came into view, and with respect to the white that dazzled round it, gave somewhat the idea of a pink flash in the glossiest white satin. Her gallant, who was a gentleman about thirty, of an immense fortune, somewhat inclined to a fatness that was in no sort displeasing, improving the hint thus tendered him of this mode of enjoyment, after settling her well in this posture and encouraging her with kisses and caresses to stand him through, drew out his affair ready erected, and whose extreme length rather disproportioned to its breadth, was the more surprising as that excess is not often the case of those of his corpulent habit. Making then the right and direct application, he drove it up to the guard, whilst the round bulge of those Turkish beauties of hers tallying with the hollow made by the bent of his belly and thighs, as they curved inwards, brought all those parts, surely not undelightfully, into warm touch and close conjunction; his hands he kept passed round her body and employed in toying with her enchanting breasts. As soon too as she felt him at home as he could reach, she lifted her head a little from the pillow, and turning her neck without much straining, but her cheeks glowing with the deepest scarlet and a smile of the tenderest satisfaction, met the kiss he pressed forward to give her, so they were thus close joined together. When leaving him to pursue his delights, she hid again her face and blushes with her hands and pillow, and thus stood passively and as favourably too as she could, whilst he kept laying at her with repeated thrusts and making the meeting flesh on both sides resound again with the violence of them. Then ever as he backened from her, we could see between them part of his long white staff foamingly in motion, till, as he went on again and closed with her, the interposing hillocks took it out of sight. Sometimes he took his hands from the semi-globes of her bosom and transferred the pressure of them to those large ones, the present subjects of his soft blockade, which he squeezed, grasped, and played with, till at length a pursuit of driving, so hotly urged, brought on the height of the fit with such symptoms of overpowering pleasure that his fair partner became now necessary to support him, panting, fainting, and dying as he discharged, which she no sooner felt the killing sweetness of than, unable to keep her legs and yielding to the mighty intoxication, she reeled, and falling forward on the couch, made it a necessity for him, if he would preserve the warm pleasurehold, to fall upon her, where they perfected, in a continued conjunction of body and ecstatatic flow, their scheme of joys for that time.

As soon as he had disengaged, the charming Emily got up, and we crowded round her with congratulations and other officious little services; for it is to be noted that, though all modesty and reserve were banished the transaction of these pleasures, good manners and politeness were inviolably observed: here was no gross ribaldry, no offensive or rude behaviour, or ungenerous reproaches to the girls for their compliance with the humours and desires of the men. On the contrary, nothing was wanting to soothe, encourage, and soften the sense of their condition to them. Men know not in general how much they destroy of their own pleasure, when they break through the respect and tenderness due to our sex, and even to those of it who live only by pleasing them. And this was a maxim perfectly well understood by these polite voluptuaries, these profound adepts in the great art and science of pleasure, who never showed these votaries of theirs a more tender respect than at the time of those exercises of their complaisance, when they unlocked their treasures of concealed beauty, and showed out in the pride of their native charms, ever more touching surely than when they parade it in the artificial ones of dress and ornament.

The frolic was now come round to me, and it being my turn of subscription to the will and pleasure of my particular elect, as well as that of the company, he came to me, and saluting me very tenderly, with a flattering eagerness, put me in mind of the compliances my presence there authorized the hopes of, and at the same time repeated to me that if all this force of example had not surmounted any repugnance I might have to concur with the humours and desires of the company, that thought the play was bespoke for my benefit, and great as his own private disappointment might be, he would suffer anything sooner than be the instrument of imposing a disagreeable task on me.

To this I answered, now without the least hesitation or mincing grimace, that, had I not even contracted a kind of engagement to be at his disposal without the least reserve, the example of such agreeable companions would alone determine me, and that I was in no pain about anything but my appearing to so great a disadvantage after such superior beauties: and take notice that I thought as I spoke. The frankness of the answer pleased them all; my particular was complimented on his acquisition and, by way of indirect flattery to me, openly envied.

Mrs Cole, by the way, could not have given me a greater mark of her regard than in managing for me the choice of this young gentleman for my master of the ceremonies; for, independent of his noble birth and the great fortune he was heir to, his person was even uncommonly pleasing, well shaped and tall; his face, marked with the smallpox, but no more than what added a grace of more manliness to features rather turned to softness and delicacy, was marvellously enlivened by eyes which were of the clearest sparkling black; in short, he was one whom any woman would, in the familiar style, readily call a very pretty fellow.

I was now handed by him to the cockpit of our match, where, as I was dressed in nothing but a white morning gown, he vouchsafed to play the male Abigail on the occasion, and spared me the confusion that would have attended the forwardness of undressing myself. My gown then was loosened in a trice, and I divested of it; my stays next offered an obstacle which quickly gave way. Louisa very readily furnishing a pair of scissors to cut the lace: off went that shell; and dropping my upper coat, I was now reduced to my under one and my shift, the open bosom of which gave the hands and eyes all the liberty they could wish. Here I imagined the stripping was to stop; but I reckoned short: my spark, at the desire of the rest, tenderly begged that I would not suffer the small remains of a covering to rob them of a full view of my whole person; and for me, who was too flexibly obsequious to dispute any point with them, and who considered the little more that remained as very immaterial, I readily assented to whatever he pleased. In an instant, then, my under petticoat was untied and at my feet, and my shift drawn over my head, so that my cap, slightly fastened, came off with it and brought all my hair

Jean-Antoine Watteau: The Toilet

down (of which, be it again remembered without vanity, I had a very fine head) in loose disorderly ringlets, over my neck and shoulders, to no unfavourable set-off of my skin.

I now stood before my judges in all the truth of nature, to whom I could not appear a very disagreeable figure, if you please to recollect what I have before said of my person, which time, that at certain periods of life robs us every instant of our charms, had, at that of mine then greatly improved into full and open bloom, for I wanted some months of eighteen. My breasts, which in the state of nudity are ever capital points, now in no more than grateful plentitude, maintained a firmness and steady independence on any stay or support that dared and invited the test of the touch. Then I was as tall, as slim-shaped as could be consistent with all that juicy plumpness of flesh ever the most grateful to the senses of sight and touch, which I owed to the health and youth of my constitution. I had not, however, so thoroughly renounced all innate shame as not to suffer great confusion at the state I saw myself in. But the whole troop round me, men and women, relieved me with every mark of applause and satisfaction, every flattering attention to praise and inspire me with even sentiments of pride on the figure I made, which, my friend gallantly protested, infinitely out-shone all other birthday finery whatever; so that, had I leave to set down, for sincere, all the compliments these connoisseurs overwhelmed me with upon this occasion, I might flatter myself with having passed my examination with approbation of the learned.

My friend however, who for this time had alone the disposal of me, humoured their curiosity, and perhaps his own, so far that he placed me in all the variety of postures and lights imaginable, pointing out every beauty under every aspect of it, not without such parentheses of kisses, such inflammatory liberties of his roving hands, as made all shame fly before them and a blushing glow give place to a warmer one of desire, which led me even to find some relish in the present scene.

But in this general survey, you may be sure, the most material spot of me was not excused the strictest visitation; nor was it but agreed that I had not the least reason to be diffident of passing even for a maid, on occasion. So inconsiderable a flaw had my preceding adventures created there, and so soon had the blemish of an over-stretch been repaired and worn out, at my age and in naturally small make in that part.

Now, whether my partner had exhausted all the modes of regaling the touch or sight, or whether he was now ungovernably wound up to strike, I know not; but briskly throwing off his clothes, the prodigious head bred by a close room, a great fire, numerous candles, and even the inflammatory warmth of these scenes induced him to lay aside his shirt too, when his breeches, before loosened, now gave up their contents to view, and showed in front the enemy I had to engage with, stiffly bearing up the port of its head unhooded and glowing red; then I plainly saw what I had to trust to: it was one of those just true-sized instruments of which the masters have a better command than the more unwieldy, inordinate sized ones are generally under. Straining me then close to his bosom, as he stood up foreright against me, and applying to the obvious niche its peculiar idol, he aimed at inserting it, which, as I forwardly favoured, he effected at once by canting up my thighs over his naked hips, and made me receive every inch, and close home; so that stuck upon the pleasure-pivot, and clinging round his neck, in which and his hair I hid my face burningly flushing with my present feelings as much as with shame, my bosom glued to his, he carried me once round the couch, on which he then, without quitting the middle-fastness or dischannelling, laid me down and began the pleasure-grist. But so provokingly predisposed and primed we were, by all the moving sights of the night, our imagination was too much heated not to melt us of the soonest; and accordingly, I no sooner felt the warm spray darted up my inwards from him, but I was punctually on flow to share the momentary ecstasy. But I had yet greater reason to boast of our harmony; for finding that all the flames of desire were not yet quenched within me but that rather, like wetted coals, I glowed the fiercer for this sprinkling, my hot-mettled spark, sympathizing with me, and loaded for a double-fire, recontinued the sweet battery with undying vigour, greatly pleased at which, I gratefully endeavoured to accommodate all my motions to his best advantage and delight. Kisses, squeezes, tender murmurs, all came into play, till our joys, growing more turbulent and riotous, threw us into a fond disorder, and, as they raged to a point, bore us far from ourselves into an ocean of boundless pleasures, into which we both plunged together in a transport of taste. Now all the impressions of burning desire, from the lively scenes I had been spectatress of, ripened by the heat of this exercise and, collecting to a head, throbbed and agitated me with insupportable irritations: I perfectly fevered and maddened with their excess. I did not now enjoy a calm of reason enough to perceive, but I, ecstatically indeed! *felt* the policy and power of such rare and exquisite provocatives as the examples of the night had proved towards thus exalting our pleasures, which, with great joy, I sensibly found my gallant shared in, by his nervous and home expressions of it: his eyes flashing eloquent flames, his action infuriated with the stings of it, all conspiring to raise my delight by assuring me of his. Lifted then to the utmost pitch of joy that human life can bear, undestroyed by excess, I touched that sweetly critical point, when, scarce prevented by the spermatic injection from my partner spurting liquid fire up to my vitals, I dissolved, and breaking out into a deep drawn sigh, sent my whole sensitive soul down to that passage where escape was denied it, by its being so deliciously plugged and choked up. Thus we lay a few blissful instants, overpowered, still, and languid; till, as the sense of pleasure stagnated, we recovered from our trance, and he slipped out of me, not, however, before he had protested his extreme satisfaction by the tenderest kiss and embrace, as well as by the most cordial expressions.

The company, who had stood round us in a profound silence, when all was over, helped me to hurry on my clothes in an instant and complimented me on the sincere homage they could not escape observing had been done (as they termed it) to the sovereignty of my charms, in my receiving a double payment of tribute at one juncture. But my partner, now dressed again, signalized, above all, a fondness unbated by the circumstance of recent enjoyment. The girls,too, kissed and embraced me, assuring me that for that time, or indeed any other, unless I pleased, I was to go through no further public trial, and that I was now consummately initiated, and one of them.

As it was an inviolable law for every gallant to keep to his partner, for the night especially, and even till he relinquished possession over to the community, in order to preserve a pleasing property and to avoid the disgusts and indelicacy of another arrangement, the company, after a short refection of biscuits and wine, tea and chocolate, served in at now about one in the morning, broke up and went off in pairs. Mrs Cole had prepared my spark and me an occasional field-bed, to which we retired, and there ended the night in one continued strain of pleasure, sprightly and uncloyed enough for us not to have formed one wish for its ever knowing an end. In the morning, after a restorative breakfast in bed, he got up, and with very tender assurances of a particular regard for me, left me to the composure and refreshment of a sweet slumber, waking out of which, and getting up to dress before Mrs Cole should come in, I found in one of my pockets a purse of guineas, which he had slipped there; and just as I was musing on a liberality I had certainly not expected, Mrs Cole came in, to whom I immediately

François Boucher: The Dark-Haired Odalisque

communicated the present, and naturally offered her whatever share she pleased. But assuring me that the gentleman had very nobly rewarded her, she would on no terms, no entreaties, no shape I could put it in, receive any part of it. Her denial she observed, was not affectation or grimace, and proceeded to read me such admirable lessons on the economy of my person and my purse as I became amply paid for my *general* attention and conformity to in the course of my acquaintance with the town. After which, changing the discourse, she fell on the pleasures of the preceding night, where I learned, without much surprise, as I began to enter her character, that she had seen everything that had passed from a convenient place, managed solely for that purpose, and of which she readily made me the confidante.

She had scarce finished with this, when the little troop of love, the girls my companions, broke in and renewed their compliments and caresses. I observed with pleasure that the fatigues and exercises of the night had not usurped in the least on the life of the complexion or the freshness of their bloom: this, I found by their confession, was owing to the management and advice of our rare directress. They went down then to figure it, as usual, in the shop; whilst I repaired to my lodgings, where I employed myself till I returned to dinner at Mrs Cole's.

Here I staid, in constant amusement, with one or other of these charming girls, till about five in the evening: when, seized with a sudden drowsy fit, I was prevailed on to go up and doze it off on Harriet's bed, who left me on it to my repose. There then I lay down in my clothes and fell fast asleep, and had now enjoyed, by guess, about an hour's rest, when I was pleasingly disturbed by one new and favourite gallant, who, inquiring for me, was readily directed where to find me. Coming then into my chamber and seeing me lie alone, with my face turned from the light towards the inside of the bed, he, without more ado, just slipped off his breeches, for the greater ease and enjoyment of the naked touch; and softly turning up my petticoat and shift behind, opened himself the prospect of the back avenue to the genial seat of pleasure; where, as I lay at my side-length, inclining rather face downward, I appeared full fair and liable to be entered. Laying himself then gently down by me, he invested me behind, and giving me to feel the warmth of his body as he applied his thighs and belly close to me, and the endeavours of that machine, whose touch has something so exquisitely singular in it, to make its way good into me, I waked, pretty much startled at first; but seeing who it was, disposed myself to turn to him, when he gave me a kiss; and desiring me to keep my posture, just lifted up my upper thigh, and ascertaining the right opening, soon drove it up to the farthest. Satisfied with which and solacing himself with lying so close in full touch of flesh in those parts, he suspended all motion, and thus steeped in pleasure, kept me lying on my side, in, to him, spoon-fashion, as he termed it, from the snug indent of the back part of my thighs, and all upwards, into the space of the bending between his thighs and belly; till, after some time, that restless and turbulent inmate, impatient by nature of longer quiet, urged him to action, which now prosecuting with all the usual train of toying, kissing, and the like, ended at length in the liquid proof on both sides that we had not been exhausted, or at least were quickly recruited of last night's draughts of pleasure on us.

With this noble and agreeable youth I lived in perfect joy and constancy. He was full bent on keeping me to himself, for the honey-month at least; but his stay in London was not even so long, his father, who had a great post in Ireland, taking him abruptly with him on his repairing thither. Yet even then I was near keeping hold of his affection and person, for he had proposed, and I had consented to follow his order to go to Ireland after him, as soon as he should be settled there; but meeting with an agreeable and advantageous match in that kingdom he chose the wiser part and forbore sending for me, but at the same time took care that I should receive a magnificent present, which did not, however, compensate for all my deep regret on my loss of him.

This event also created a chasm in our little society, which Mrs Cole, on the foot of her usual caution, was in no haste to fill up. But then it redoubled her attention to procure me in the advantages of the traffic for a counterfeit maidenhead, some consolation for the sort of widowhood I had been left in; and this was a scheme she had never lost prospect of, and only waited for a proper person to bring it to bear with.

But I was, it seems, fated to be my own caterer in this, as I had been in my first trial of the market.

I had now passed near a month in the enjoyment of all the pleasures of familiarity and society with my companions, whose particular favourites (the baronet excepted, who soon after took Harriet home) had all, on the terms of community established in the house, solicited the gratification of their taste for variety in my embraces. But I had with the utmost art and address, on various pretexts, eluded their pursuit without giving them cause to complain: and this reserve I used neither out of dislike to them or disgust of the thing, but my true reason was my attachment to my own, and my tenderness of invading the choice of my companions who, outwardly exempt, as they seemed, from jealousy, could not but in secret like me the better for the regard I had for, without making a merit of it, to them. Thus easy, and beloved by the whole family, did I go on, when one day that, about five in the afternoon, I stepped over to a fruiterer's shop in Covent-Garden to pick some table fruit for myself and the young women, I met with the following adventure.

Gainsborough: Study of a Woman

Whilst I was chaffering for the fruit I wanted, I observed myself followed by a young gentleman, whose rich dress first attracted my notice; for the rest, he had nothing remarkable in his person, except that he was pale, thin-made, and ventured himself upon legs rather of the slenderest. Easy was it to perceive, without seeming to perceive it, that it was me he wanted to be at, by his making a full set at and keeping his eyes fixed on me, till he came to the same basket that I stood at, and cheapening, or rather giving the first price asked for the fruit, began his approaches. Now most certainly I was not at all out of figure to pass for a modest girl, I had neither the feathers nor *fumet* of a tawdry town-miss; a straw hat, a white gown, clean linen, and above all, a certain natural and easy air of modesty (which the appearances of never forsook me, even on those occasions that I most broke in upon it in practice) were all signs that gave him no opening to conjecture my condition. He spoke to me, and this address from a stranger, throwing a blush into my cheeks that still set him wider off the truth, I answered him with an awkwardness and confusion the more apt to impose as there was really a mixture of the genuine in them. But when proceeding, on the foot of having broken the ice, to join discourse, he went into other leading questions, I put so much innocence, simplicity, and even childishness into my answers that on no better foundation, liking my person as he did, I will answer for it that he would have been sworn for my modesty. There is, in short, in the men, when once they are caught by the eye especially, a fund of gullibility that their lordly wisdom little dreams of, and in virtue of which the most sagacious of them are seen so often our dupes. Amongst other queries he put to me, one was whether I was married. I replied that I was too young to think of that this many a year. To that of my age, I answered, and sunk a year upon him, passing myself for not seventeen. As to my way of life, I told him I had served an apprenticeship to a milliner in Preston and was come to town after a relation that I found, on my arrival, was dead, and I now lived journey-woman to a milliner in town. That last article indeed was not much on the side of what I pretended to pass for; but it did pass, under favour of the growing passion I had inspired him with. After he had next got out of me, very dextrously as he thought, what I had no sort of design to make a reserve of, my own, my mistress's name, and place of abode, he loaded me with fruit, all the rarest and dearest he could pick out, and sent me home, pondering on what might be the consequence of this adventure.

As soon then as I came to Mrs Cole's I related to her all that had passed, on which she very judiciously concluded that, if he did not come after me there was no harm done and that, if he did, as her presage suggested to her he would, his character and his views should be well sifted, so as to know whether the game was worth the springs, that in the meantime nothing was easier than my part in it, since no more rested on me than to follow her cue and promptership throughout, to the last act.

The next morning, after an evening spent on his side, as we afterwards learnt, in perquisitions into Mrs Cole's character in the neighbourhood (than which nothing could be more favourable to her designs upon him), my gentleman came in his chariot to the shop, where Mrs Cole alone had an inkling of his errand. Asking then for her, he easily made a beginning of acquaintance by bespeaking some millinery ware, when, as I sat without lifting up my eyes, and pursuing the hem of a ruffle with the utmost composure and simplicity of industry, Mrs Cole took notice that the first impressions I made on him ran no risk of being destroyed by those of Louisa and Emily, who were then setting at work with me. After vainly endeavouring to catch my eyes in rencounter with his, as I held my head down, affecting a kind of consciousness of guilt for having, by speaking to him, given him encouragement and means of following me home, and after giving Mrs Cole direction when to bring herself the things home, and the time he should expect them, he went out, taking with him some goods that he paid for liberally, for the better grace of his introduction.

The girls all this time did not in the least smoke the mystery of this new customer; but Mrs Cole, as soon as we were conveniently alone, insured me, in virtue of her long experience in these matters, that for this bout my charms had not missed fire; for that by his eagerness, his manner and looks, she was sure he had it. The only point now in doubt was his character and circumstances, which her knowledge of the town would soon gain her sufficient acquaintance with, to take her measures upon.

And effectively, in a few hours, her intelligence served her so well that she learned that this conquest of mine was no other than Mr Norbert, a gentleman originally of a great fortune, which, with a constitution naturally not the best, he had greatly impaired by his over-violent pursuit of the vices of the town, in the course of which, having worn out and staled all the more common modes of debauchery, he had fallen into a state of maiden-hunting, in which chase he had ruined a number of girls, sparing no expense to compass his ends, and generally using them well till tired, or cooled by enjoyment, or springing a new face, he could with more ease disembarrass himself of the old ones, and resign them up to their fate, as his sphere of achievements of that sort lay only amongst such as he could proceed with by way of bargain and sale.

Concluding from these premises, Mrs Cole observed that a character of this sort was ever lawful prize; that the sin would be not to make the best of our market of him; and that she thought such a girl as me only too good for him at

Rowlandson: An Irish Member on his way to the House of Commons

any rate, and on any terms.

She went then, at the hour appointed, to his lodgings in one of our Inns of Court, which were furnished in a taste of grandeur that had a special eye to all the conveniences of luxury and pleasure. Here she found him ready waiting, and after finishing her business of pretence, and a long circuit of discussions concerning her trade, which she said was very bad, the qualities of her servants, 'prentices, journey-women, the discourse naturally landed at length on me, when Mrs Cole, acting admirably the good old prating gossip, who lets everything escape her when her tongue is set in motion, cooked him up a story so plausible of me, throwing in every now and then such strokes of art, with all the simplest air of nature, in praise of my person and temper as finished him finely for her purpose; whilst nothing could be better counterfeited than her innocence of his. But when now fired and on edge, he proceeded to drop hint of his design and views upon me, after he had with much confusion and pains brought her to the point (she kept as long aloof from as she though proper) of understanding him, without now affecting to pass for a dragoness of virtue by flying out into those violent and ever suspicious passions, she stuck with a better grace and effect to the character of a plain, honest, good sort of a woman, that knew no harm, and that, getting her bread in an honest way, was made of easy and flexible stuff enough to be wrought upon to his ends by his superior skill and address. But, however, she managed so artfully that three or four meetings took place before he could obtain the least favourable hope of her assistance, without which, he had, by a number of fruitless messages, letters, and other direct trials of my disposition, convinced himself there was no coming at me, all which too raised at once my character and price with him.

Regardful, however, of not carrying these difficulties to such a length as might afford time for starting discoveries or incidents unfavourable to her plan, she at last pretended to be won over by mere dint of entreaties, promises and, above all, the the dazzling sum she took care to wind him up to the specification of, when it was now even a piece of art to feign, at once, a yielding to the allurements of a great interest, as a pretext for her yielding at all, and the manner of it such as might persuade him she had never before dipped her virtuous finger in a affair of that sort.

Thus she led him through all the gradations of difficulty and obstacles necessary to enhance the value of the prize he aimed at; and in conclusion, he was so struck with the little beauty I was mistress of, and so eagerly bent on gaining his ends of me, that he left her even no room to boast of her management in bringing him up to her mark, he drove so plum of himself into everything tending to make him swallow the bait. Not that in other respects Mr Norbert was not clear-sighted enough, not that he did not perfectly know the town, and even by experience, the very branch of imposition now in practice upon him; but we had his passion to friend so much, he was so blinded and hurried on by it that he would have thought any undeception a very ill office done to his pleasure. Thus concurring, even precipitantly, to the point she wanted him at, Mrs Cole brought him at last to hug himself on the cheap bargain he considered the purchase of my imaginary jewel was to him, at no more than three hundred guineas to myself, and a hundred to the brokeress; being a slender recompense for all her pains, and all the scruples of conscience she had now sacrificed to him for this the first time of her life: which sums were to be paid down on the nail, upon livery of my person, exclusive of some not inconsiderable presents that had been made in the course of the negotiation: during which I had occasionally, but sparingly, been introduced into his company, at proper times and hours, in

Unknown: Introduction (detail)

which it is incredible how little it seemed necessary to string my natural disposition to modesty higher, in order to pass it upon him for that of a very maid. All my looks and gestures ever breathing nothing but that innocence which the men so ardently require in us, for no other end than to feast themselves with the pleasure of destroying it, and which they are so grievously, with all their skill, subject to mistakes in.

When the articles of the treaty had been fully agreed on, the stipulated payments duly secured, and nothing now remained but the execution of the main point, which centered in the surrender of my person up to his free disposal and use, Mrs Cole managed her objections, especially to his lodgings, and insinuations so nicely, that it became his own mere motion and urgent request that this copy of a wedding should be finished at her house. At first indeed, she did not care, not she, to have such doings in it – she would not for a thousand pounds have any of the servants or 'prentices know it – her precious good name would be gone for ever – with the like excuses: however, on superior objections to all other expedients whilst she took care to start none but those that were most liable to them, it came round at last to the necessity of her obliging him in that conveniency, and of doing a little more where she had already done so much.

The night then was fixed, with all possible respect to the eagerness of his impatience, and in the meantime Mrs Cole had omitted no instructions, nor even neglected any preparation that might enable me to come off with honour, in regard to the appearance of virginity, except that, favoured as I was by nature, with all the narrowness of stricture in that part requisite to conduct my designs, I had no occasion to borrow those auxiliaries of art that create a momentary one, easily discovered by the test of a warm bath; and as to the usual bloody symptoms of defloration, which, if not always, are generally attendants on it, Mrs Cole had made me the mistess of an invention of her own, which could hardly miss its effect, and of which more in its place.

Everything then being disposed and fixed for Mr Norbert's reception, he was at the hour of eleven at night, with all the mysteries of silence and secrecy, let in by Mrs Cole herself, and introduced into her bedchamber, where, in an old-fashioned bed of hers, I lay fully undressed and panting, if not with the fears of a real maid, at least with those perhaps greater of a dissembled one, which gave me an air of confusion and bashfulness that maiden-modesty had all the honour of, and was indeed scarce distinguishable from it, even by less partial eyes than those of my lover, so let me call him, for I ever thought the term *cully* too cruel a reproach to the men for their abused weakness for us.

As soon as Mrs Cole, after the old gossipery, on those occasions, used to young women abandoned for the first time to the will of man, had left us alone in her room, which, by the by, was well lighted up, at his previous desire, that seemed to bode a stricter examination than he afterwards made. Mr Norbert, still dressed, sprung towards the bed, where I had got my head under the clothes, and defended them a good while before he could even get at my lips, to kiss them: so true it is, that a false virtue, on this occasion, ever makes a greater rout and resistance than a true one! From thence he descended to my breasts, the feel of which I disputed tooth and nail with him, till tired with my resistance, and thinking probably to give a better account of me when got into bed to me; he hurried his clothes off in an instant, and came into bed.

Meanwhile, by the glimpse I stole of him, I could easily discover a person far from promising any such doughty performances as the storming of maidenheads generally requires, and whose flimsy consumptive texture gave him more the air of an invalid that was pressed than of a volunteer on such hot service.

At scarce thirty, he had already reduced his strength of appetite down to a wretched dependance on forced provocatives, very little seconded by the natural powers of a body jaded and wracked off to the lees by constant repeated overdraughts of pleasure, which had done the work of sixty winters on his springs of life, leaving him at the same time all the fire and heat of youth in his imagination, which served at once to torment and to spur him down the precipice.

As soon as he was in bed, he threw off the bedclothes, which I suffered him to force from my hold, and I now lay as exposed as he could wish, not only to his attacks, but his visitation of the sheets, where, in the various agitations of my body, through my endeavours to defend myself, he could easily assure

Hogarth: Before (detail)

himself there was no preparation or stain of blood, though, to do him justice, he seemed less strict an examinant than I had apprehended from so experienced a practitioner. My shift then he fairly tore open, finding I made too much use of it to barricade my breasts as well as the more important avenue. Yet in everything else he proceeded with all the marks of tenderness and regard to me, whilst the art of my play was to show none for him. I acted then all the niceties, apprehensions, and terrors supposable for a girl perfectly innocent to feel at so great a novelty as a naked man in bed with her for the first time. He scarce even obtained a kiss but what he ravished; I put his hand away twenty times from my breasts, where he had satisfied himself of their hardness and consistence with passing for hitherto unhandled goods. But when grown impatient for the main point, he now threw himself upon me, and first trying to examine me with his finger, sought to make himself further way, I complained of his usage bitterly: I thought he would not have served a body so. I was ruined – I did not know what I had done – I would get up, so I would, and at the same time kept my thighs so fast locked that it was not for a strength like his to force them open or do any good. Finding thus my advantages, and that I had both my own and his motions at command, the deceiving him became so easy that it was perfect playing upon velvet. In the meantime, his machine, which was one of those sizes that slip in and out without being minded, kept pretty stiffly bearing against that part which the shutting my thighs barred access to; but finding, at length, he could do no good by mere dint of bodily strength, he resorted to entreaties and arguments; to which I only answered, with a tone of shame and timidity, that I was afraid it would kill me – Lord! – I would not be served so – I was never so used in all my born days – I wondered he was not ashamed of himself, so I did – With such silly infantile moods of repulse and complaint as I judged best adapted to express the characters of innocence, and fright. Pretending, however, to yield at length to the vehemence of his insistence, in action and words, I sparingly disclosed my thighs, so that he could just touch the cloven inlet with the tip of his instrument, but as he fatigued and toiled to get it in, a twist of my body, so as to receive it obliquely, not only thwarted his admission, but, giving a scream as if he had pierced me to the heart, I shook him off me, with such violence that he could not with all his might to it keep the saddle. Vexed indeed at this he seemed, but not in the style of any displeasure with me for my skittishness; on the contrary, I dare swear he held me the dearer and hugged himself for the difficulties that even hurt his

Jean-Honoré Fragonard: The Bolt (*detail*)

instant pleasure. Fired, however, now, beyond all bearance of delay, he remounts and begged of me to have patience, stroking and soothing me to it by all the tenderest endearments and protestations of what he would moreover do for me, at which, feigning to be something softened, and abating of the anger that I had shown at his hurting me so prodigiously, I suffered him to lay my thighs aside, and make way for a new trial; but I watched the directions and management of his point so well that no sooner was the orifice in the least open to it, but I gave such a timely jerk as seemed to proceed, not from the evasion of his entry, but from the pain his efforts to it put me to: a circumstance too that I did not fail to accompany with proper gestures, sighs, and cries of complaint, of which, that he had hurt me – he killed me – I should die – were the most frequent interjections. But now, after repeated attempts, in which he had not made the least impression towards gaining his point, at least for that time, the pleasure rose so fast upon him that he could not check or delay it, and in the vigour and fury, which the approaches of the height of it inspired him, he made one fierce thrust that had almost put me by my guard, and lodged it so far that I could feel the warm inspersion just within the exterior orifice, which I had the cruelty not to let him finish there, but threw him out again, not without a most piercing loud exclamation, as if the pain had put me beyond all regard of being overheard. It was easy then to observe that he was more satisfied, more highly pleased, with the supposed motives of his balk of consummation than he would have been at the full attainment of it. It was on this foot that I salved to myself all the falsity I employed to procure him that blissful pleasure in it, which most certainly he would not have tasted in the truth of things. Eased, however, and relieved by one discharge, he now applied himself to soothe, encourage, and put me into humour and patience to bear his next attempt, which he began to prepare and gather force for, from all the incentives of the touch and sight which he could think of, by examining every individual part of my whole body, which he declared his satisfaction with in raptures of applause, kisses universally imprinted, and sparing no part of me, in all the eagerest wantonnesses of feeling, seeing and toying. His vigour, however, did not return so soon, and I felt him more than once pushing at the door but so little in a condition to break in that I question whether he had the power to enter, had I held it ever so open. But this he then thought me too little acquainted with the nature of things to have any regret or confusion about, and he kept fatiguing himself and me for a long time before he was in any state of stiffness to resume his attempts with any prospect of success. And then I breathed him so warmly, and kept him so at bay, that before he had made any sensible progress in point of penetration he was deliciously sweated and wearied out indeed, so that it was deep in the morning before he had achieved his second let-go, about half way of the entrance, I all the time crying and complaining of his prodigious vigour, and the immensity of what I appeared to suffer splitting up with. Tired, however, at length, with such athletic drudgery, my champion began now to give out and to gladly embrace the refreshment of some rest. Kissing me then with much affection, and recommending me to my repose, he presently fell fast asleep; which, as soon as I had well satisfied myself of, I, with much composure of body, so as not to wake him by any motion, with much ease and safety, too, played off Mrs Cole's device for perfecting the signs my virginity.

In each of the head bedposts, just above where the bedsteads are inserted into them, there was a small drawer so artfully adapted to the mouldings of the timber-work that it might have escaped even the most curious search; which drawers were easily opened or shut by the touch of a spring, and were fitted each with a shallow glass tumbler full of a prepared fluid blood; in which lay soaked, for ready use, a sponge that required no more than gently reaching the hand to it, taking it out, and properly squeezing between the thighs, when it yielded a great deal more of the red liquid than would save a girl's honour; after which, replacing it, and touching the spring, all possibility of discovery or even of suspicion is taken away; and all this was not the work of the fourth part of a minute, and on whichever side one lay, the thing was equally easy and practicable by the double care taken to have each bedpost provided alike. True it is that, had he waked and caught me in the fact, it would at least have covered me with shame and confusion; but then, that he did not, was with the precautions I took, a risk of a thousand to one in my favour.

At ease now, and out of all fear of any doubt or suspicion on his side, I addressed myself in good earnest to my repose, but could obtain none. And in about half an hour's time, my gentleman waked again, and turning towards me, I feigned a sound sleep, which he did not long respect; but girding himself again to renew the onset, he began to kiss and caress me, when now making as if I just waked, I complained of the disturbance and of the cruel pain that this little rest had stolen my senses from. Eager, however, for the pleasure as well as honour of consummating an entire triumph over my virginity, he said and did everything that could overcome my resistance, and bribe my patience to the end, which now I was ready to listen to, from being secure of the bloody proofs I had prepared of his victorious violence, though I still thought it good policy not to let him in yet a while. I answered then only to his importunities in sighs and moans that I was so hurt, I could not bear it – I was sure he had done me a mischief; that he had, – he was such a sad man! Turning, at this, down the clothes, and viewing the field of battle by the glimmer of a dying taper, he saw plainly my thighs, shift and sheets, all yet wet and stained with what he readily took for virgin gore, proceeding from his last half-penetration: convinced and transported at which, nothing could equal his joy and exultation. The illusion was complete; no other conception entered his head but that of his having been at work upon an unopened mine, which idea, upon so strong an evidence, redoubled at once his tenderness for me and his ardour for breaking it wholly up. Kissing me then with the utmost rapture, he comforted me, and begged my pardon for the pain he had put me to, observing, withal, that it was only a thing in course, but the worst was certainly past, and that with a little courage and constancy I should get it once well over, and never after experience anything but the greatest pleasure. By little and little I suffered myself to be prevailed on, and giving, as it were, up the point to him, I made my thighs, insensibly spreading them, yield him liberty of access, which, improving, he got a little within me, when, by a well managed reception, I worked the female screw so nicely that I kept him from the easy mid-channel direction, and, by dexterous wreathings and contortions, creating an artifical difficulty of entrance, made him win it inch by inch, with the most laborious struggles, I all the time sorely complaining, till at length, with might and main, winding his way in, he got it completely home, and giving my virginity, as he thought, the *coup de grâce*, furnished me the cue of setting up a terrible outcry, whilst he, truimphant and like a cock clapping his wings over his down-trod mistress, pursued his pleasure, which presently rose, in virtue of this idea of a complete victory, to a pitch that made me soon sensible of his melting period, whilst I now lay acting the deep wounded, breathless, frightened, undone, no longer maid.

You will ask me, perhaps, whether all this time I enjoyed any perception of pleasure? I assure you, little or none; till just towards the latter end, a faintish sense of it came on mechanically, from so long a struggle and frequent fret in that ever sensible part. But, in the first place, I had no taste for the person I was suffering the embraces of, on a purely mercenary account, and then I was not entirely delighted with myself for the jade's part I was playing, whatever excuses I might have to plead for being brought into it; but then this insensibility kept me so much the mistress of my mind and motions that I could the better manage so close a counterfeit, through the whole scene of deception.

Recovered at length to more show of life, by his tender condolences, kisses, and embraces, I upbraided him and reproached him for my ruin, in such natural terms as added to his satisfaction with himself for having accomplished it; and guessing, by certain observations of mine, that it would be rather favourable to him to spare him, when he sometime after, feebly enough, came on again to the assault, I resolutely withstood any further endeavours, on a pretext that flattered his prowess, of my being so violently hurt and sore that I could not possibly endure a fresh trial. He then graciously granted me a respite, and the morning soon after advancing, I got rid of further importunity, till Mrs Cole, being rung for by him, came in, and was made acquainted, in terms of the utmost joy and rapture, with his triumphant certainty of my virtue, and the finishing stroke he had given it, in the course of the night; of which, he added, she would see proof enough, in bloody characters, on the sheets.

You may guess how a woman of her turn of address and experience humoured the jest and played him off with mixed exclamations of shame, anger, compassion for me, and of her being pleased that all was so well over; in which last, I believe, she was perfectly sincere. And now, as the objection (which she had represented as an invincible one) to my lying the first night at his lodgings (which were studiously calculated for a freedom of intrigues), on the account of my maiden fears and terrors at the thoughts of going to a gentleman's chambers, and being alone with him in bed, was surmounted, she pretended to persuade me, in favour to him, that I should go there to him, whenever he pleased, and still keep up all the necessary appearances of working with her, that I might not lose, with my character, the prospect of getting a good husband, and at the same time her house would be kept the safer from scandal. All this seemed so reasonable, so considerate, to Mr Norbert that he never once perceived that she did not want him to resort to her house, lest he might in time discover certain inconsistencies with the character she had set out with to him; besides that this plan greatly flattered his own ease and views of liberty.

Leaving me then to my much wanted rest, he got up, and Mrs Cole, after settling with him all points relating to me, got him undiscovered out of the house. After which, and I was awake, she came in and gave me due praises on my success. Behaving, too, with her usual moderation and disinterestness, she refused any share of the sum I had thus earned and put me into such a secure and easy way of disposing of my affairs, which now amounted to a kind of little fortune, that a child of ten years old might have kept the account and property of them safe in its hands.

I was now restored again to my former state of a kept mistress, and used punctually to wait on Mr Norbert at his chambers whenever he sent a messenger for me, which I constantly took care to be in the way of, and managed with so much caution that he never once penetrated the nature of my connexions with Mrs Cole; but indolently given up to ease and the town dissipations, the perpetual hurry to them hindered him from looking into his own affairs, much less into mine.

In the meantime, if I may judge from my own experience, none are better paid or better treated during their reign than the mistresses of those who, enervated by nature, debaucheries, or age, have the least employment for the sex: sensible that a woman must be satisfied some way, they ply her with a thousand little tender attentions, presents, caresses, confidences, and exhaust their invention in means and devices to make up for the capital deficiency; and even towards lessening that, what arts, what modes, what refinements of pleasure have they not recourse to, to raise their languid powers and press nature into the service of their sensuality! But here is their misfortune, that, when by a course of teasing, worrying, handling, wanton postures, lacivious motions, they have at length accomplished a flashy enervated enjoyment, they have at the same time lighted up a flame in the object of their passion that, not having the means themselves to quench, drives her for relief into the next person's arms, who can finish their work: and thus they become bawds to some secret favourite, tried and approved of for a more vigorous and satisfactory execution; for with women, of our turn especially, however well our hearts may be disposed, there is a controlling part, or queen-seat in us, that governs itself by its own maxims of state, amongst which not one is stronger in practice with it than, in matter of its dues, never to accept the will for the deed.

Mr Norbert, who was much in this ungracious case, though he professed and showed to like me extremely, could but seldom consummate the main joy itself with me, without such a length and variety of preparations as were at once wearisome and inflammatory.

Sometimes he would strip me stark naked on a carpet, by a good fire; when he would contemplate me almost by the hour, disposing me in all the figures and attitudes of body that it was susceptible of being viewed in; kissing me in every part, the most secret and critical one so far from excepted that it received most of that branch of homage. Then his touches were so exquisitely

Rowlandson: Undressing by the Fire

wanton and luxuriously diffused, and penetrative at times, that he made me perfectly rage with titillating fires, when, after all, and with much ado, he had gained a short-lived erection, he would perhaps melt it away in a washy sweat, or a premature abortive effusion, that provokingly mocked my eager desires; or, if carried home, how faltered and unnervous the execution! how insufficient the sprinkle of a few heat-drops to extinguish all the flames he had kindled.

One evening I cannot help remembering, that, returning home from him with a spirit he had raised in a circle his wand had proved too weak to lay, as I turned the corner of a street, I was overtaken by a young sailor. I was then in that spruce, neat, and plain dress, which I ever affected, and perhaps might have in my trip a certain air of restlessness unknown to the composure of cooler thoughts. However, he seized me a prize, and, without ceremony, threw his hands round my neck, and kissed me boisterously and sweetly. I looked at him with a beginning of anger and indignation at his rudeness, that softened away into other sentiments as fast I viewed him: for he was tall, manly-carriaged, handsome of body and face, so that I ended my stare with asking him, in a tone turned to tenderness, what he meant. At which, with the same frankness and vivacity as he had begun with me, he proposed treating me with a glass of wine. Now, certain it is that, had I been in a calmer state of blood than I was; had I been less under the dominion of unappeased irritations and desires, I should have refused him without hesitation. But I do not know how it was, my pressing calls, his figure, the occasion, and, if you will, the powerful combination of all these, with a start of curiosity to see the end of an adventure so novel to me as being thus treated like a common street-plyer, made me give a silent consent: in short, it was not my head that I now obeyed. I suffered myself then to be towed along, as it were, by this man-of-war, who took me under his arm as familiarly as if he had known me all his lifetime, and led me into the next convenient tavern, where we were shown into a little room on one side of the passage. Here scarce allowing himself patience till the drawer brought in the wine called for, he fell directly on board me; when, untucking my handkerchief and giving me a smacking buss, he laid my breasts bare at once, which he handled with that keenness of gust that bridges a ceremonial ever more tiresome than pleasing on such pressing occasions; and now hurrying towards the main point, we found no conveniency for our purpose, two or three disabled chairs, and a rickety table composing the whole furniture of the room.

Without more ado, he plants me with my back standing against the wall, and my petticoats up; and coming out with a splitter indeed, made it shine, as he brandished it, in my eyes, and going to work with an impetuosity and eagerness, bred very likely by a long fast at sea, went to give me the taste of it. I straddled, I humoured my posture, and did my best in short to buckle to it; I took part in it too. But still things did not jee to his thorough liking: changing then in a trice his system of battery, he leads me to the table, and with a

Thomas Rowlandson: Jack Tar Admiring the Fair Sex

Unknown: Bachelor's Fare

master-hand lays my head down on the edge of it, and with the other canting up my petticoat and shift, bared my naked posteriors to his blind and furious guide. It forces its way between them, and I feeling pretty sensibly that it was not going by the right door and knocking desperately at the wrong one, I told him of it: 'Pooh,' says he, 'my dear, any port in a storm.' Altering, however, directly his course, and lowering his point, he fixed it right, and driving it up with a delicious stiffness, made all foam again and gave me the *tout* with such fire and spirit that in the fine disposition I was in when I submitted to him, and stirred up so fiercely as I was, I got the start of him, and went away into the melting swoon; and squeezing him, whilst in the convulsive grasp of it, drew from him such a plenteous bedewal of balmy sweets as joined to my own effusion, perfectly floated those parts, and drowned in a deluge all my raging conflagration of desire.

When this was over, how to make my retreat was my concern; for, though I had been so extremely pleased with the difference between this warm broadside, poured so briskly into me, and the tiresome pawing and toying to which I had owed the unappeased flames that had driven me into this step, now I was grown cooler, I began to apprehend the danger of contracting an acquaintance with this however agreeable stranger; who, on his side, spoke of passing the evening with me and continuing our intimacy, with an air of determination that made me afraid of it being not so easy to get away from him as I could wish. In the meantime I carefully concealed my uneasiness, and readily pretended to consent to stay with him, telling him I should only step to my lodgings to leave a necessary direction, and then instantly return. This he very glibly swallowed, on the notion of my being one of those unhappy street-errants who devote themselves to the pleasure of the first ruffian that will stoop to pick them up, and, of course, that I would scarce bilk myself of my hire, by not returning to make the most of the job. Thus he parted with me, not before, however, he had ordered, in my hearing, a supper which I had the barbarity to disappoint him of my company to.

But when I got home, and told Mrs Cole my adventure, she represented so strongly to me the nature and dangerous consequences of my folly, the risks to my health in being so open-legged and free of my flesh, that I not only took resolutions never to venture so rashly again, which I inviolably preserved, but passed a good many days in continual uneasiness lest I should have met with other reasons, besides the pleasure of that rencounter, to remember it. But these fears wronged my pretty sailor, for which I gladly make him this reparation.

I had now lived with Mr Norbert near a quarter of a year, in which space I circulated my time very pleasantly between my amusements at Mrs Cole's and a proper attendance on that gentleman, who paid me profusely for the unlimited complaisance with which I passively humoured every caprice of pleasure, and which had won upon him so greatly that, finding, as he said, all that variety in me alone which he had sought for in a number of women, I had made him lose his taste for inconstancy and new faces. But what was yet at least as agreeable to me as his fondness and attachment, as well as much more flattering: the love I had inspired him with bred a deference to me that was of great service to his health. For having by degrees, and with most pathetic representations, brought him to some husbandry of it, and to ensure the duration of his pleasures by moderating their use and correcting those excesses in them he was so addicted to, and which had shattered his constitution and destroyed his powers of life in the very point for which he seemed chiefly desirous to live, he was grown more delicate, more temperate, and all in course more healthy; his gratitude for which was taking a turn very favourable for my fortune, when once more the caprice of it dashed the cup from my lips.

His sister Lady L – , for whom he had a great affection, desiring him to accompany her down to Bath for her health, he could not refuse her such a favour, and accordingly, though he counted on staying away from me no more than a week at farthest, he took his leave of me with an ominous heaviness of heart, and left with me a sum far above the state of his fortune and very inconsistent with the intended shortness of his journey; but it ended in the longest that can be, and is never but once taken: for, arrived at Bath, he was not there two days before he fell into a debauch of drinking with some gentlemen that threw him into a high fever which carried him off in four days' time, never once out of a delirium. Had he been in his senses to make a will, perhaps he might have made favourable mention of me in it. Thus, however, I lost him; and as no condition of life is more subject to revolutions than that of a woman of pleasure, I soon recovered my cheerfulness, and now beheld myself once more struck off the list of kept mistresses and returned into the bosom of the community from which I had been in some manner taken.

Mrs Cole, still continuing her friendship, offered me her assistances and advice towards another choice; but I was now in a state of ease and affluence

Rowlandson: Mrs Barry, the old Bawd

enough to look about me at leisure; and so to any constitutional calls of pleasure, their pressure or sensibility was greatly lessened by a consciousness of the ease with which they were to be satisfied at Mrs Cole's house, where Louisa and Emily still continued in the old way; and my great favourite, Harriet, used often to come and see me, and entertain me, with her head and heart full of the happiness she enjoyed with her dear baronet, whom she loved with tenderness and constancy, even though he was her keeper and, what is yet more, had made her independent by a handsome provision for her and hers.

After various further encounters and adventures, Louisa and Emily both leave Mrs Cole, for a lover and a husband respectively.

These desertions had, however, now so far thinned Mrs Cole's cluck that she was left with only me, like a hen with one chicken. But though she was earnestly entreated and encouraged to recruit her *corps*, her growing infirmities, and above all the tortures of a stubborn hip-gout, which she found would yield to no remedy, determined her to break up her business, and retire with a decent pittance into the country, where I promised myself nothing so sure as my going down to live with her, as soon as I had seen a little more of life and improved my small matters into a competency that would create me an independence on the world; for I was now, thanks to Mrs Cole, wise enough to keep that essential in view.

Thus I was then to lose my preceptress, as did the philosophers of the town the white crow of their profession; for, besides that she never ransomed her customers, whose taste too she ever studiously consulted; besides that she never racked her pupils with unconscionable extortions, nor ever put their hand earnings, as she called them, under the contribution of poundage, she was a severe enemy to the seduction of innocence, and confined her acquisitions solely to the unfortunate young women who, having lost it, were but the juster objects of compassion. Amongst these, indeed, she picked out such as suited her views, and taking them under her protection, rescued them from the danger of the public sinks of ruin and misery, to place or form them, well or ill, in the manner you have seen. Having then settled her affairs, she set out on her journey. after taking the most tender leave of me and, at the end of some excellent instructions, recommending me to myself, with an anxiety, perfectly maternal: in short, she affected me so much that I was not presently reconciled to myself for suffering her, at any rate, to go without me; but fate had, it seems otherwise disposed of me.

I had, on my separation from Mrs Cole, taken a pleasant convenient house near Marylebone, but easy to rent and manage, from its smallness; which I furnished neatly and modestly. There, with a reserve of eight hundred pounds, the fruit of my deference to Mrs Cole's counsels, exclusive of clothes, some jewels, some plate, I saw myself in purse for a long time, to wait without impatience for what the chapter of accidents might produce in my favour.

Here, under the new character of a young gentlewoman whose husband was gone to sea, I had marked me out such lines of life and conduct as, leaving me at a competent liberty to pursue my views, either of pleasure or fortune, bounded me nevertheless strictly within the rules of decency and discretion: a disposition in which you cannot escape observing a true pupil of Mrs Cole's.

I was scarce, however, well warm in my new abode when, going out one morning pretty early to enjoy the freshness of it, in the pleasing outlet of the fields, accompanied only by a maid whom I had hired; as we were carelessly walking among the trees, we were alarmed with the noise of a violent coughing: turning our heads towards which, we distinguished a plain well-dressed elderly gentleman, who, attacked with a sudden fit, was so much overcome as to be forced to give way to it and sit down at the foot of a tree, where he seemed suffocating with the severity of it, being perfectly black in the face. Not less moved than frightened with which, I flew on the instant to his relief, and using the rote of practice I had observed on the like occasion, I loosened his cravat, and clapped him on the back; but whether to any purpose, or whether the cough had had its course, I know not; but the fit went immediately off; and now recovered to his speech, and legs, he returned me thanks, with as much emphasis as if I had saved his life. This naturally engaging a conversation, he acquainted me where he lived, which was a considerable distance from where I met with him, and where he strayed insensibly on the same intention of a morning walk.

He was, as I afterwards learned in the course of the intimacy which this little accident gave birth to, an old bachelor turned of sixty, but of a fresh, vigorous complexion, insomuch that he scarce marked five and forty, having never racked or forced his constitution, by permitting his desires to overtax his ability.

As to his birth and condition, his parents, honest and failed mechanics, had, by the best traces he could get of them, left him an infant orphan on the parish; so that it was from a charity school that, by honesty and industry, he made his way into a merchant's counting-house; from whence, being sent to a house in Cadiz, he there, by his talents and activity, acquired a fortune, but an immense one; with which he returned to his native country, where he could not, however, so much as fish one single relation out of the obscurity he was born in. Taking then a taste for retirement, and pleased to enjoy life, like a mistress in the dark, he flowed his days in all the ease of opulence, without the least parade of it, and rather studying the concealment than the show of a fortune, looking down on a world he perfectly knew; himself, to his wish unknown and unmarked by it.

But as I propose to devote a letter entirely to the pleasure of retracing to you all the particulars of my acquaintance with this ever, to me, memorable friend, I shall, in this transiently touch on no more than may serve as mortar to cement, or form the connexion of my history, and to obviate your surprise that one of my high blood and relish of life should count a gallant of three score such a catch.

Referring then to a more explicit narrative, to explain by what progressions our acquaintance, certainly innocent at first, insensibly changed nature, and ran into unplatonic lengths, as might well be expected from one of my condition of life, and above all from that principle of electricity which scarce ever fails of producing fire, when the sexes meet. I shall only here acquaint you that, as age had not subdued his tenderness for our sex, neither had it robbed him of the powers of pleasing, since whatever he wanted in the bewitching charms of youth, he atoned for or supplemented with the advantages of experience, the sweetness of his manners, and, above all, his flattering address in touching the heart by an application to the understanding. From him it was that I first learned to any purpose, and not without infinite pleasure, that I had such a portion of me worth bestowing some regard on; from him I received my first essential encouragement, and instructions, how to put it into that train of cultivation which I have since pushed to the little degree of improvement you see it at; he it was who first taught me to be sensible that the pleasures of the mind were superior to those of the body, at the same time that they were so far from obnoxious to, or incompatible with each other that, besides the sweetness in the variety and

François Boucher: Woman Fastening Her Garter, with Her Maid (*detail*)

transition, the one served to exalt and perfect the taste of the other to a degree that the senses alone can never arrive at.

Himself a rational pleasurist, as being much too wise to be ashamed of the pleasures of humanity, loved me indeed, but loved me with dignity, in a mean equally removed from that sourness of forwardness which age is unpleasingly characterised by, and from that childish silly dotage that so often disgraces it, and which he himself used to turn into ridicule and compare to an old goat affecting the frisk of a young kid.

In short, everything that is generally unamiable in his season of life was, in him, repaired by so many advantages that he existed a proof manifest, at least to me, that it is not out of power of age to please, if it lays out to please, and if, making just allowances, those in that class do not forget that it must cost them more pains and attention than what youth, the natural spring time of joy, stands in need of: as fruits out of season require proportionably more skill and cultivation to force them.

With this gentleman then, who took me home soon after our acquaintance commenced, I lived near eight months, in which time, my constant complaisance, my docility, my attention to deserve his confidence and love, and a conduct, in general, devoid of the least art and founded on my sincere esteem and regard for him, won and attached him so firmly to me that, after having generously trusted me with a genteel, independent settlement, proceeding to heap marks of affection on me, he appointed me, by an authentic will, his sole heiress and executrix; a disposition which he did not outlive two months, being taken from me by a violent cold that he contracted as he unadvisedly ran to the window, on an alarm of fire, at some streets' distance, and stood there naked-breasted and exposed to the fatal impressions of a damp night-air.

After acquitting myself of my duty towards my deceased benefactor, and paying him a tribute of unfeigned sorrow, which a little time changed into the most tender, grateful memory of him that I shall ever retain, I grew somewhat comforted by the prospect that now opened to me, if not of happiness, at least of affluence and independence.

I saw myself then, in the full bloom and pride of youth (for I was not yet nineteen), actually at the head of so large a fortune as it would have been even the height of impudence in me to have raised my wishes, much more my hopes, to; and that this unexpected elevation did not turn my head, I owed to the pains my benefactor had taken to form and prepare me for it, as I owed his opinion of my management of the vast possessions he left me to what he had observed of the prudential economy I had learned under Mrs Cole, of which the reserve he saw I had made as a proof and encouragement to him.

But alas! how easily is the enjoyment of the greatest sweets in life, in present possession, poisoned by the regret of an absent one! But my regret was a mighty and a just one, since it had my only truly beloved Charles for its object.

Given him up I had indeed completely, having never once heard from him since our separation: which, as I found afterwards, had been my misfortune, and not his neglect, for he wrote me several letters which had all miscarried; but forgotten him I never had: and amidst all my personal infidelities, not one had made a pin's point impression on a heart impenetrable to the true love-passion, but for him.

As soon, however, as I was mistress of this unexpected fortune, I felt more than ever how dear he was to me, from its insufficiency to make me happy, whilst he was not to share it with me. My earliest care, consequently, was to endeavour at getting some account of him. But all my researches produced me no more light than that his father had been dead some time, not so well as even with the world, and that Charles had reached his port of destination in the South Seas, where, finding the estate he was sent to recover dwindled to a trifle, by the loss of two ships, in which the bulk of his uncle's fortune lay, he was come away with the small remainder, and might perhaps, according to the best advice, in a few months return to England, from whence he had, at the time of this my inquiry, been absent two years and seven months: a little eternity in love!

You cannot conceive with what joy I embraced the hopes thus given me of seeing the delight of my heart again; but as the term of months was assigned it, in order to divert and amuse my impatience for his return, after settling my affairs with much ease and security, I set out on a journey for Lancashire, with an equipage suitable to my fortune, and with a design purely to revisit my place of nativity, for which I could not help retaining a great tenderness, and might naturally not be sorry to show myself there, to the advantage I was now in pass to do, after the report Esther Davis had spread of my being spirited away to the Plantations, for on no other supposition could she account for the suppression of my self to her, since her leaving me so abruptly at the inn. Another favourite intention I had, to look out for my relations, though I had none besides distant ones, and to prove a benefactress to

Hogarth: A Country Inn Yard (detail)

them. Then Mrs Cole's place of retirement, lying in my way, was not amongst the least of the pleasures I had proposed to myself in this expedition.

I had taken nobody with me but a discreet decent woman, to figure it as my companion, besides my servants, and was scarce got into an inn, about twenty miles from London, where I was to sup and pass the night, when such a storm of wind and rain sprang up as made me congratulate myself on having got under shelter before it began.

This had continued a good half hour when, bethinking me of some directions to be given to the coachman, I sent for him, and not caring that his shoes should soil the very clean parlour in which the cloth was laid, I stepped into the hall-kitchen, where he was, and where, whilst I was talking to him, I slantingly observed two horsemen driven in by the weather, and both wringing wet; one of whom was asking if they could be assisted with a change, till their clothes could be dried. But heavens! who can express what I felt at the sound of a voice, ever present to my heart, and that it now rebounded at! or when pointing my eyes towards the person it came from, they confirmed its information, in spite of so long an absence, and of a dress one would have imagined studied for a disguise: a horseman's great coat with a stand-up cape, and his hat flapped; but what could escape the piercing alertness of a sense surely guided by love? A transport then, like mine, was above all consideration or schemes of surprise, and I, that instant, with the rapidity of the emotions that I felt the spur of, shot into his arms, crying out as I threw mine round his neck: 'My life! – my soul! – my *Charles*!' and, without further power of speech, swooned away under the oppressing agitations of joy and surprise.

Recovered out of my entrancement, I found myself in my charmer's arms, but in the parlour, surrounded by a crowd which this event had gathered round us, and which immediately, on a signal from the discreet landlady, who currently took him for my husband, cleared the room, and desirably left us alone to the raptures of this reunion, my joy at which had like to have proved, at the expense of my life, its power superior to that of grief at our fatal separation.

The first object then that my eyes opened on as their supreme idol, and my supreme wish, Charles, on one knee, holding me fast by the hand and gazing at me in a transport of fondness. Observing my recovery, he attempted to speak, and give vent to his impatience of hearing my voice again, to satisfy him once more that it was me; but the mightiness and suddenness of the surprise continuing to stun him, choked his utterance. He could only stammer out a few broken, half-formed, faltering accents, which my ears greedily drinking in, spelt, and put together so as to make out their sense: 'After so long! – so cruel! – an absence, – my dearest *Fanny*! – Can it? Can it be you? –' stifling me at the same time with kisses that, stopping my mouth, at once prevented the answer that he panted for, and increased the delicious disorder in which all my senses were rapturously lost. Amidst, however, this crowd of ideas, and all blissful ones, there obtruded only one cruel doubt, that poisoned nearly all this transcendent happiness; and what was it but my dread of his being too excessive to be real! I trembled now with the fear of its being no more than a dream, and of my waking out of it into the horror of finding it one: under this fond apprehension, imagining I could not make too much of the present prodigious joy before it should vanish and leave me in the desert again, nor verify its reality too strongly, I clung to him, I clasped him, as if to hinder him from escaping me again. 'Where have you been? – how could you, could you leave me? – Say you are still mine – that you still love me, – and thus! thus!' (kissing him as if I would consolidate lips with him) 'I forgive you – forgive my hard fortune in favour of this restoration.' All these interjections breaking from me, in that wildness of expression that justly passes for eloquence in love, drew from him all the returns my fond heart could wish or require. Our caresses, our questions, our answers, for some time, observed no order; all crossing or interrupting one another in sweet confusion, whilst we exchanged hearts at our eyes, and renewed the ratifications of a love unabated by time or absence: not a breath, not a motion, not a gesture on either side but what was strongly impressed with it. Our hands, locked in each other, repeated the most passionate squeezes, so that their fiery thrill went to the heart again.

Thus absorbed, and concentered in this unutterable delight, I had not attended to the sweet author of it being thoroughly wet and in danger of catching cold; when, in good time, the landlady, whom the appearance of my equipage (which, by the by, Charles knew nothing of) had gained me an interest in, for me and mine, interrupted us by bringing in a decent shift of linen and clothes, which now, somewhat recovered into a calmer composure by the coming in of a third person, I pressed him to take the benefit of, with a tender concern and anxiety that made me tremble for his health.

The landlady leaving us again, he proceeded to shift, in the act of which, though he proceeded with all that modesty which became these first solemner instants of our re-meeting, after so long an absence, I could not contain certain snatches of my eyes, lured by the dazzling discoveries of his naked skin, that escaped him as he changed his linen, and which I could not observe the unfaded life and complexion of without emotions of tenderness and joy, that had himself too purely for their object to partake of a loose or mis-timed desire.

He was soon dressed in these temporary clothes, which neither fitted him nor became the light my passion placed him in, to me at least. Yet as they were on him, they looked extremely well, in virtue of that magic charm which love put into everything that he touched or had relation to him, and where indeed was that dress that a figure like his would not give grace to? For now, as I eyed him more in detail, I could not but observe the even favourable alteration which the time of his absence had produced in his person.

There were still the same exquisite lineaments, still the same vivid vermillion and bloom reigning in his face, about now the roses were more fully blown: the tant of his travels and a beard somewhat more distinguishable had, at the expense of no more delicacy than what he could better spare than not, given it an air of becoming manliness and maturity that symmetrized nobly with that air of distinction and empire with which nature had stamped it, in a rare mixture with the sweetness of it. Still nothing had he lost of that smooth plumpness of flesh which, flowing with freshness, blooms florid to the eye and delicious to the touch; then, his shoulders were grown more square, his shape more formed, more portly, but still free and airy. In short, his figure showed riper, greater, and perfecter to the experienced eye than in his tender youth; and now, he was not much more than two and twenty.

In this interval, however, I picked out of the broken, often pleasingly interrupted account of himself that he was, at that instant, actually on his road to London, in not a very paramount plight or condition, having been wrecked on the Irish coast, for which he had prematurely embarked, and lost the little all he had brought with him from the South Seas, so that he had not, till after great shifts and hardships in the company of his fellow traveller, the captain, got so far on his journey; that so it was (having heard of his father's death and circumstances), he had now the world to begin again, on a new account; a situation, which, he assured me, in a vein of sincerity that, flowing from his heart, penetrated mine, gave him no farther gain than that he had it not in his power to make me as happy as he could wish. My fortune, you will please to observe, I had not entered upon any overture of, reserving to feast myself with the surprise of it to him in calmer instants. And as to my dress, it could give him no idea of the truth, not only as it was mourning but likewise in a style of plainness and simplicity that I have ever kept to with studied art. He pressed me indeed tenderly to satisfy his ardent curiosity, both with regard to my past and present state of life since his being torn away from me. But I had the address to elude his questions by answers that, showing his satisfaction at no great distance, won upon him to waive his impatience in favour of the thorough confidence he had in my not delaying it; but for respects should in good time acquaint him with.

Charles, however, thus returned to my longing arms, tender, faithful, and in health, was already a blessing too mighty for my conception! But, Charles in distress! – Charles reduced and broken down to his naked personal merit, was such a circumstance, in favour of the sentiments I had for him, as exceeded my utmost desires. And, accordingly, I seemed so visibly charmed, so out of time and measure pleased at his mention of his ruined fortune that he could account for it no way but that the joy of seeing him again had swallowed up every other sense or concern.

In the meantime, my woman had taken all imaginable care of Charles's travelling companion; and, as supper was coming in, he was introduced to me, when I received him as became my regard for all of Charles's acquaintances or friends.

We four then supped together in the style of joy, congratulation, and pleasing disorder that you may guess. For my part, though all these agitations had left me not the least stomach but for that uncloying feast, the sight of my adored youth, I endeavoured to force it, by way of example for him, who, I conjectured, must want such a recruit after riding, and, indeed, he ate like a traveller, but gazed at and addressed me all the time like a lover.

After the cloth was taken away, and the hour of repose came on, Charles and I were, without further ceremony, in quality of man and wife, shown up together to a very handsome apartment, and, all in course, the bed, they said, to be the best in the inn.

And here, decency forgive me! if, once more I violate the laws and, keeping the curtains undrawn, sacrifice thee for the last time to that confidence, without reserve, with which I engaged to recount to you the most striking circumstances of my youthful disorders.

As soon then as we were in the room together, left to ourselves, the sight of the bed starting the remembrance of our first joys, and the thought of my being instantly to share it with the dear possessor of my virgin heart, moved me so strongly that it was well I leaned upon him, or I must have fainted again, under the overpowering sweet alarm. Charles saw into my confusion, and forgot his own, that was scarce less, to apply himself to the removal of mine.

But now the true refining passion had regained thorough possession of me, with all its train of symptoms; a sweet sensibility, a tender timidity, love-sick yearnings, tempered with diffidence and modesty, all held me in a subjection of soul incomparably dearer to me than the liberty of heart which I had been long, too long! the mistress of, in the course of those grosser gallantries, the consciousness of which now made me sigh with a virtuous confusion and regret. No real virgin, in short, in view of the nuptial bed, could give more

L. Leopold Boilly: The Sweet Awakening

bashful blushes to unblemished innocence than I did to a sense of guilt; and indeed I loved Charles too truly not to feel severely that I did not deserve him.

As I kept hesitating and disconcerted under this soft distraction, Charles, with a fond impatience, took the pains to undress me, and all I can remember amidst the flutter and discomposure of my senses was some fluttering exlcamations of joy and admiration, more especially at the feel of my breasts, now set at liberty from my stays, and which, panting and rising in tumultuous throbs, swelled upon his dear touch, and gave it the welcome pleasure of finding them well formed and unfailed in firmness.

I was soon laid in bed, and scarce languished an instant for the darling partner of it, before he was undressed and got between the sheets, with his arms clasped round me, giving and taking, with a gust inexpressible, a kiss of welcome that my heart, rising to my lips, stamped with its warmest impression, concurring to my bliss with that delicate and voluptuous emotion which Charles alone had the secret to excite, and which constitutes the very life, the essence of pleasure.

Meanwhile, two candles lighted on a side-table near us, and a joyous wood-fire, threw a light into the bed that took from one sense, of great importance to our joys, all pretext of complaining of its being shut out of it share of them: and indeed, the sight of my idolized youth was alone, from the ardour with which I had wished for it, without other circumstance, a pleasure to die of.

But as action was now a necessity to desires so much on edge as ours, Charles, after a very short prelusive dalliance, lifting up my linen and his own, laid the broad treasures of his manly chest close to my bosom, both beating with the tenderest alarms; when now the sense of his glowing body in naked touch with mine, took all power over my thoughts out of my own disposal, and delivered up every faculty of my soul to the sensiblest of joys that, affecting me infinitely more with my distinction of the person than of the sex, now brought my conscious heart deliciously into play; my heart, which, eternally constant to Charles, had ever taken any part in my occasional sacrifices to the calls of constitution, complaisance or interest. But,ah! what became of me, when, as the powers of solid pleasure thickened upon me, I could not help feeling the stiff stake that had been adorned with the trophies of my despoiled virginity bearing hard and inflexible against one of my thighs, which I had not yet opened, from a true principle of modesty revived by a passion too sincere to suffer any aiming at the false merit of difficulty, or my putting on an impertinent mock-coyness.

I have, I believe, somewhere before remarked that the feel of that favourite piece of manhood has, in the very nature of it, something inimitably pathetic. Nothing can be dearer to the touch, or can affect it with a more delicious sensation. Think then! as a lover thinks, what must be the consummate transport of that quickest of our senses, in their central seat too! when, after so long a deprival, it felt itself reinflamed under the pressure of that peculiar scepter-member which commands us all, but especially my darling elect from the face of the whole earth. And now, at its mightiest point of stiffness, it felt to me something so subduing, so active, so solid, and agreeable that I know not what name to give its singular impression; but the sentiment of consciousness of its belonging to my supremely beloved youth gave me so pleasing an agitation and worked so strongly on my soul that it sent all its sensitive spirits to that organ of bliss in me dedicated to its reception. There concentering to a point, like rays in a burning glass, they glowed, they burnt with the intensest heat; the springs of pleasure were, in short, wound up to such a pitch, I panted now with so exquisitely keen an appetite for the imminent enjoyment, that I was even sick with desire, and unequal to support the combination of two distinct ideas that delightfully distracted me! For all the thought I was capable of was that I was now in touch at once with the instrument of pleasure and the great-seal of love; ideas that, mingling streams, poured such an ocean of intoxicating bliss on a weak vessel, all too narrow to contain it, that I lay overwhelmed, absorbed, lost in an abyss of joy, and dying of nothing but immoderate delight.

Charles then roused me somewhat out of this ecstatic distraction with a complaint softly murmured, amidst a crowd of kisses, at the position, not so favourable to his desires, in which I received his urgent insistence for admisssion, where that insistence was alone so engrossing a pleasure that it made me inconsistently suffer a much dearer one to be kept out. But how sweet to correct such a mistake! My thighs, now obedient to the intimations of love and nature, gladly disclose, and with a ready submission resign up the lost gateway to entrance at pleasure: I see! I feel! the delicious velvet tip! – he enters might and main with – oh! – my pen drops from me here in the ecstasy now present to my faithful memory! Description, too deserts me and delivers over a task, above its strength of wing, to the imagination; but it must be an imagination exalted by such a flame as mine, that can do justice to that sweetest, noblest of all sensations that hailed and accompanied the stiff insinuation all the way up, till it was at the end of its penetration, sending up, through my eyes, the sparks of the love-fire that ran all over me, and blazed in every vein and every pore of me: a system incarnate of joy all over.

I had now totally taken in love's true arrow, from the point up to the feather, in that part where, making no new wound, the lips of the original one of nature, which had owed its first breathing to this dear instrument, clung, as if sensible of gratitude, in eager suction round it, whilst all its inwards embraced it tenderly with a warmth of gust, a compressive energy, that gave it, in its way, the heartfelt welcome in nature; every fibre there gathering tight round it, and straining ambitiously to come in for its share of the blissful touch.

As we were giving then a few moments of pause to the delectation of the senses, in dwelling with the highest relish on this intimatest point of reunion, and chewing the cud of enjoyment, the impatience natural to the pleasure soon drove us into action. Then began the driving tumult on his side, and the responsive heaves on mine, which kept me up to him; whilst, as our joys grew too mighty for utterance, the organs of our voices, voluptuously intermixing, became organs of the touch. And, oh, that touch, how delicious! how poignantly luscious! – And now! now! I felt to the heart of me, I felt the prodigious keen edge with which love, presiding over this act, points the pleasure. Love! that may be styled the Attic salt of enjoyment: and indeed, without it, the joy, great as it is, is still a vulgar one, whether in a king or a beggar; for it is undoubtedly love alone that refines, ennobles, and exalts it.

Thus happy then, by the heart, happy by the senses, it was beyond all power, even of thought, to form the conception of a greater delight than what I was now consummating the fruition of.

Charles, whose whole frame all convulsed with the agitation of his rapture, whilst the tenderest fires trembled in his eyes, all assured me of a perfect concord of joy, penetrated me so profoundly, touched me so vitally, took me so much out of my own possession, whilst he seemed himself so much in mine that in a delicious enthusiasm I imagined such a transfusion of heart and spirit as that, coaliting and making one body and soul with him, I was him, and he, me.

But all this pleasure, tending, like life from its first instants, towards its own dissolution, lived too fast not to bring on upon the spur its delicious moment of mortality; for presently the approach of the tender agony discovered itself by its usual signals, that were quickly followed by my dear love's liquid emanation of himself, that spun out and shot feelingly indeed up

Thomas Rowlandson: The Country Squire New Mounted

Fragonard: Love Scene

the ravished indraught, where the sweetly soothing balmy titillation opened at the warm jerk all the sluices of joy on my side, which, ecstatically in flow, helped to allay the prurient glow, and drowned our pleasure for a while, soon, however, to be on float again! For Charles, true to nature's laws, in one breath expiring and ejaculating, languished not long in the dissolving trance, but, recovering spirit again, soon gave me to feel that the true mettle springs of his instrument of pleasure were by love, and perhaps by a long vacation, wound up too high to be let down by a single explosion: his stiffness still stood my friend. Resuming then the action afresh, without dislodging or giving me the trouble of parting from my sweet tenant, we played over again the same opera, with the same delightful harmony and concert; our ardours, like our love, knew no remission. And, all as the tide served, my lover, lavish of his stores and pleasure-milked, overflowed me once more from the fullness of those his oval reservoirs of the genial emulsion; whilst, on my side, a convulsive grasp, in the instant of my giving down my liquid contribution, rendered me sweetly subservient at once to the increase of his joy and if its effusions, moving me so as to make me exert all those springs of the compressive exsuction, with which the sensitive mechanism of that part thirstily draws and drains the nipple of love, with much such an instinctive eagerness and attachment as, to compare great with less, kind nature engages infants at the breast, by the pleasure they find in the motion of their little mouths and cheeks to extract the milky stream prepared for their nourishment.

But still there was no end of his vigour, this double discharge had so far from extinguished his desires, for that time, that it had not even calmed them. And, at his age, desires are power: he was proceeding then, amazingly, to push it to a third triumph, still without uncasing. If a tenderness, natural to true love, had not inspired me with self-denial enough to spare, and not over strain him, and, accordingly, entreating him to give himself and me quarter, I obtained at length a short suspension of arms, but not before he had exultingly satisfied me that he gave out standing.

The remainder of the night, with what we borrowed upon the day, we employed with unwearied fervour in celebrating thus the festival of our re-meeting, and got up pretty late in the morning, gay, brisk, and alert, though rest had been a stranger to us; but the pleasures of love had been to us what the joy at victory is to an army: repose, refreshment, everything.

The journey into the country being now entirely out of the question, and

William Hogarth: The Happy Marriage

orders having been given overnight for turning the horses' heads towards London, we left the inn as soon as we had breakfasted, not without a liberal distribution of the tokens of my grateful sense of the happiness I had met within it.

Charles and I were in my coach, the captain and my companion in a chaise hired purposely for them, to leave us the conveniency of a tête-à-tête.

Here, on the road, as the tumult of my senses was tolerably composed, I had command enough of head to break properly to him the course of life that the consequences of my separation from him had driven me into, which, at the same time that he tenderly deplored with me, he was the less shocked at as, on reflecting how he had left me circumstanced, he could not be entirely unprepared for it.

But when I opened the state of my fortune to him, and with that sincerity which, from me to him, was so much a nature in me, I begged of him his acceptance of it, on his own terms, I should appear to you perhaps too partial to my passion, were I to attempt the doing his delicacy justice. I shall content myself then with assuring you that, after his flatly refusing the unreserved, unconditional donation that I long persecuted him in vain to accept, it was at length, in obedience to his serious commands (for I stood out unaffectedly, till he exerted the sovereign authority which love had given him over me), that I yielded my consent to wave the remonstrance I did not fail of making strongly to him, against his degrading himself and incurring the reflection, however unjust, of having, for respects of fortune, bartered his honour for infamy and prostitution, in making one his wife who thought herself too much honoured in being but his mistress.

The plea of love then overruling all objections, Charles, entirely won with the merit of my sentiments for him, which he could not but read the sincerity of in a heart ever open to him, obliged me to receive his hand, by which means I was in pass, amongt other innumerable blessings, to bestow a legal parentage on those fine children you have seen by this happiest of matches.

Thus, at length, I got snug into port, where, in the bosom of virtue, I gathered the only uncorrupt sweets: where, looking back on the course of vice I had run, and comparing its infamous blandishments with the infinitely superior joys of innocence, I could not help pitying, even in point of taste, those who, immersed in a gross sensuality, are insensible to the so delicate charms of *Virtue*, than which even *Pleasure* has not a greater friend, nor than *Vice* a greater enemy. Thus temperance makes men lords over those pleasures that intemperance enslaves them to: the one, parent of health, vigour, fertility, cheerfulness, and every other desirable good in life; the other, of diseases, debility, barrenness, self-loathing, with only every evil incident to human nature.

You laugh perhaps at this tail-piece of morality, expressed from me by the force of truth resulting from compared experiences: you think it, no doubt, out of place; out of character; possibly, too, you may look on it as the paltry finesse of one who seeks to mask a devotee to vice under a rag of a veil, impudently smuggled from the shrine of virtue; just as if one was to fancy oneself completely disguised at a masquerade, with no other change of dress than turning one's shoes into slippers; or as if a writer should think to shield a treasonable libel by concluding it with a formal prayer for the king. But, independent of my flattering myself that you have a juster opinion of my sense and sincerity, give me leave to represent to you that such a supposition is even more injurious to virtue than to me, since, consistently with candour and good nature, it can have no foundation but in the falsest of fears, that its pleasures cannot stand in comparison with those of vice, but let truth dare to hold it up in its most alluring light: then mark! how spurious, how low of taste, how comparatively inferior its joys are to those which virtue gives sanction to, and whose sentiments are not above making even a sauce for the sense, but a sauce of the highest relish; whilst vices are the harpies that infect, and foul the feast. The paths of vice are sometimes strewed with roses, but then they are for ever infamous for many a thorn, for many a cankerworm; those of virtue are strewed with roses purely, and those eternally unfading ones.

If you do me then justice, you will esteem me perfectly consistent in the incense I burn to virtue: if I have painted vice all in its gayest colours, if I have decked it with flowers, it has been solely in order to make the worthier, the solemner, sacrifice of it to virtue.

You know Mr C – O – , you know his estate, his worth, and good sense; can you, will you pronounce it ill meant, at least of him, when, anxious for his son's morals, with a view to form him to virtue, and inspire him with a fixed, a rational contempt for vice, he condescended to be his master of the ceremonies, and led him by the hand through the most noted bawdy-houses in town, where he took care that he should be familiarized with all the scenes of debauchery so fit to nauseate a good taste? The experiment, you will cry, is dangerous. True – on a fool; but are fools worth the least attention to?

I shall see you soon, and in the meantime think candidly of me, and believe me ever.

Madam,
Yours, &c. &c. &c.

François Boucher: Woman at her Toilet